THE LUSTS OF HIS
BODY FIRED HIS
THIRST FOR FREEDOM

She was on the earth and she wore nothing
and her legs had been pushed apart.
His hands touched her breasts knowingly, and
her nipples hardened to his touch.
His hands were everywhere. She was gasping.
It was hard for her to see anything
until the moment when that black presence
hovered over her.

He was nearly stopped by the look of welcome
mixed with fear that he saw on her face.
This was the moment to which she had been
building herself, and in a while there
would be no turning back . . .

ROGUE SLAVE

LIONEL WEBB

WILDSIDE PRESS

PART ONE

CHAPTER 1

The two girls were fighting. The tall girl shouted and cursed as she reached for the short one, trying to get her off balance or to get a grip on the shorter girl's frizzy hair.

"I'll get you," the tall one shouted. "You won't have him! You won't."

The short one suddenly whispered, "I've had him already and I'm going to keep him."

The tall one tried to punch her for that. The black women who were watching the two fighters and had formed a circle suddenly let out a cheer that was followed by a groan from those who were rooting for the tall girl to win. The women wore kerchiefs to keep their heads from the broiling Alabama sun, and the kerchiefs glinted as they moved. There wasn't a man in sight.

The short one was trying to rip the tall one's clothes off her body. She couldn't get a grip on them, though, and the years she had spent picking cotton had made her nails so short that she couldn't scratch.

She suddenly leaned forward into the tall one and pulled off a button and some cloth with it. The tall girl's clothes looked crumpled now as well as cheap and dirty.

As the short girl got a grip on a part of the tall one's frayed blouse, the tall girl suddenly punched her in the arm. The short girl had to pull away, taking the clothes with her. The arm flew, as if there wasn't a person at the other end of it, and crashed into the sturdy trunk of a tree. The short girl shrieked in pain.

"Bitch!" the tall one called out. "Two-legged whore bitch!"

"Bitch yourself," the short one said, through teeth wet against pain.

There was a commotion at the end of the area in which the girls were fighting. Heavy footsteps could be heard on the earth and then a pair of black hands formed a fence, almost, between the two girls. The hands wouldn't be moved, and neither girl could take a step forward.

"You might both get hurt this way," the black man said softly. "It's lucky that Mister Joe is on the other side right now, so you can both go back to work."

Mister Joe was the plantation overseer, a calm man who could stand almost anything except laziness or sloppy work. Since he saw a considerable amount of both kinds from the slaves who didn't have much to lose, he was a calm man who spent a good deal of time getting upset.

The black man asked softly, "Are you hurt?"

The tall girl started to say, "No," and the short girl said pluckily, "I'll be all right, Hannibal." It was the short girl who had been asked the question.

The black man asked, "What's wrong, Miriam?"

"My hand," Miriam said. "But it'll be all right."

"What's wrong with the hand? Come on, tell me."

"It crashed into a tree and it sort of went cr-runch."

"Can you make a fist with it?"

She tried, but it wasn't strong.

"That's bad. If there's no way to hide it, Mister Joe will see it and say that you can't work any more. You know what that'll mean, Miriam."

The short girl looked down.

Hannibal raised his voice to take in the women in the circle. "One of you will have to help her with the work. Who?"

6

Hannibal waited for some answer. He was a six-footer with skin as black as tar. Muscles rippled when he moved, and he hardly ever seemed to make a move that wasn't graceful. He wore a dark shirt and pants that had been cut off just below the knees, showing powerful calves. There was a feeling of strength in his every move, as well as instinctive grace.

"Well?" he asked the crowd again. "Who'll help my gal here?"

A girl called out, "Sarah Jane works right next to Miriam."

The tall girl threw her head back, like a horse getting a bit in its mouth for the first time. "If *she* asks me to help her," Sarah Jane said briskly, "I'll think about it. I wouldn't say yes or no, but I'll think about it."

Miriam began, "I think I'd die before I got down on my knees in front of that—"

"Quiet, gal," Hannibal rumbled. He turned to the tall girl. "Nobody asks, Sarah Jane. I'm telling you to do what my Miriam needs done, less'n you want a busted arm, too."

Sarah Jane heard the cackling in the audience. Her dark face flushed.

"You wouldn't hurt me," she said, unbelievingly.

"If you bet on that, Sarah Jane, you're going to lose whatever you put up."

"If I have to, I'll do it," Sarah Jane agreed sullenly. She looked at Miriam, who had lost the fight but won the man. She looked down at herself. "I need something to wear. I can't work like this."

Her blouse had been ripped open part way, allowing a dark breast to swing free and in sight.

"Mister Joe won't let me work like this." Sarah Jane looked maliciously over at Miriam. "You've got another blouse, haven't you, gal?"

Miriam said nothing, even though both girls knew the answer. The other blouse was the one that she planned on wearing the next time she and Hannibal were together. It was a special blouse, and only for Hannibal to see.

"You can't have it," Miriam said automatically.

It was Hannibal who settled the argument. "She needs it, Miriam. Give it to her."

Miriam hung her head in surrender. The tall girl suddenly threw her head back and laughed.

There was a sound of slurring, a sound that came from just beyond the circle. It was as if several sets of footsteps had moved across the dirt. Then snickering was heard, and Hannibal whirled around in time to see a horse's rump moving away in the opposite direction and the capped blonde hair of the white girl who sat astride the horse.

"That was Miss Leola," he said grimly, "Master Dudley's daughter. If she heard about the busted arm, Miriam, then she'll tell somebody and you'll be sold down the river for sure."

Miriam shivered.

Leola Stark had indeed heard some shouted words about one of the nigger gals having a broken arm, but a sight she had never seen before in her life had simply driven the recollection out of her head. She was still dazed, and she felt lucky she wasn't walking or she'd probably have fallen down because her legs would have suddenly not been able to hold her.

At the age of nineteen, Leola Stark was, on the surface, very much like any other well-brought-up girl in the southern states in this year of 1846. She had a clear skin and was fashionably slight. She was style-conscious, and never let a year go by without getting a new wardrobe directly from Paris. She could sew, but not very well. She could knit after a fashion. She could play the piano, but only light and simple pieces. Occasionally, she would accompany herself, but her voice was shaky and uncer-

8

tain. She longed to speak French like a native, but found the lessons difficult. With Italian, her experience was very much the same. It was hoped that early next year, like any young lady in her station of life, Leola Stark would make the Grand Tour of Europe.

At Safe Harbor plantation, she indulged herself in an occasional petty vice. She had a weakness for racy French novels, for instance, but her difficulties with the language made it nearly impossible for her to fully appreciate what she read. Without her parents' knowledge she used mammarian cream, which was supposed to make the breasts bigger, but in Leola's case there was no reason under the hot sun why the cream should be needed.

Until just a few moments ago, truth to tell, she had been colossally bored. She had taken Buttercup out for her usual morning canter, taking into account the fact that Buttercup had a weakness for going near the slave quarters; she was tended by blacks and saw them more often than whites, so she felt some affection for the blacks of Safe Harbor.

Leola herself had certainly never felt any attraction for the colored folk on the plantation. The bucks were short and weedy. They never worked, it seemed. Joe Everdine, the overseer, was always telling about them somehow making corn liquor or sour mash and reeling around drunk. According to Daddy, a lot of bucks escaped on the so-called underground railroad to a freedom which they spent in laying around drunk and becoming public charges and having kids as fast as rabbits did.

A few moments ago, though, attracted by the noise of two darkie gals in a fight, she had seen the big black boy who broke them up. Never in life had she seen such a handsome buck. Big and dark black and with muscles that gleamed as if they had been covered with oil. Every move he made was lovely to see. Everything he did, she felt sure, would be just beautiful to watch.

9

She had stared at him until the horse suddenly made some noise and then an impulse had prodded her into turning the horse around and starting out of there.

Not till she was halfway across the quiet restful field did she realize that she had no idea of the slave's name. To her own sudden surprise, she was determined to find out who he was and to see him again This time, though, she would want to look at him much more closely.

Dudley Stark said, "This is nonsense!"

He slammed the newspaper down and realized at the same time that he had chomped one end of his Havana cigar disagreeably out of shape. He spat it out, hurled it into the tray provided for that purpose, and whirled on his wife again.

Dudley Stark was considered a short-tempered man, and he was generally known as being on such a short fuse that if he kept his temper it was a surprise to others and people thought that he might not be well. He was expected to lose his temper at the first sign of something going wrong and he usually obliged people in that way. It would have embarrassed him to be told that he wasn't a cruel man by the standards of his time, and that in fact he had more kindness in him than did most of his peers.

He was an inch below six feet and in his forties. He had gray hair and a dollop of mustache that looked as if it had been sprayed across his upper lip. He dressed well, drank more moderately than his friends, and knew how to hold his liquor if he had indeed taken a few drops too many.

Now, sober as a judge, he pointed at the offending newspaper as he whirled on his wife.

"Do they honestly think they're going to make us do without slaves?" he demanded. "These Senators and Congressmen in Washington are disgusting, always getting set to debate slavery and 'expose' it for what they think it is. Meanwhile, they put an owner's nerves on edge for nothing at all."

"I suppose that's true, dear," Nettie Stark said. She had been a beauty as the youngest of the Briggs girls and she was an older beauty now. She was always so tidy that it gave Dudley considerable pleasure just to look at her.

"Of course it's true," Dudley said, a little more mildly than he had intended. "If they should really pass an idiot law abolishing slavery, the South would secede and those dunderheads in Washington know it very well . . . oh, hello, dear."

His daughter had come into the parlor. Leola, dressed for supper in fine spun silk with dark lace at the throat, swayed with every motion as she walked. She looked very much like Nettie as a young girl.

"Did I hear you say something about slavery?" Leola asked with more sharpness than she had probably intended.

"More about the Congress," Dudley Stark began, then stopped himself. "What makes you ask? Since when are you taking an interest in business matters?"

"I'm always interested in the plantation."

"You? Generally you spend all your time thinking about how much you hate it here at Safe Harbor and how much you wish you were on tour in Europe."

Leola shrugged. "I suppose that the Congress is asking questions about slavery again. You always take on like that when they do. Does the Congress want to know if our slaves are well-fed?"

"Certainly our darkies are well-fed. What put an idea like that into your head?"

"I was riding Buttercup on the fields today and all the slaves I saw seemed a little scrawny. You don't think that Joe is starving them, do you?"

"Joe Everdine is a good man, and as for you—well, your grandfather Stark and your great-grandfather Stark would

11

be ashamed at hearing such talk from somebody who's got their name."

"I was only wondering if we feed our slaves well."

"Sure we do." Dudley snorted. "Slaves don't eat much 'cause they don't need so much to work. They don't hardly *do* no work except make malt liquor on the side."

"But I don't think we have a single slave who looks well-fed or heavy," Leola persisted. "Not one."

"Don't you wonder if our darkies are doing good by us? Do you just worry about how we're doing to them?"

"Daddy, I was just curious." Softly she added, "There's hardly anything else to do around Safe Harbor except be curious."

"All right, all right, Leola, I've heard that nothing-else-to-do business from you before." He glanced irritably at his wife. "Isn't it time we ate?"

"It will be in a few moments, I'm sure," Nettie murmured.

"Unless our daughter wants us to take what we've got and bring it down to the darkie quarters."

Leola, as stubborn as her father, said, "All I tried to tell you is that I haven't seen one well-fed slave at Safe Harbor. There isn't one strong, husky-looking—"

"There certainly is," Dudley bridled. "Nobody's going to tell me I don't feed my slaves."

"Who is he, then?" Leola asked. "I'll bet five dollars that there isn't one. There couldn't be even one."

Dudley rummaged in his memory, recollecting Hannibal but for some reason he didn't understand not wanting to mention that muscular brute of a darkie. Some reason or other.

He grinned. "Well, you look at Rufus sometime soon, and you'll change your mind. Ask Joe Everdine to show you Rufus and then you can see for yourself."

He didn't understand that sudden soft smile curving

Leola's mouth and why it should be so disturbing. "Rufus. I'll remember that name."

"He's big, Rufus is. Big as this house."

The outer door opened on Josh, the elderly house slave. He wore a black frock coat, like a deacon, and pants to match. He was gray and walked with a stoop, but Dudley and Nettie could remember when he had been in his thirties and spry as a billy goat.

"Supper is ready," he said, leaving out their titles as he generally did. Nettie couldn't break him of the habit and had given up trying. "Vittles is on the table."

"We'll be right there, Josh," Nettie said firmly. "Leola, please go in first."

Their daughter did. Dudley turned to his wife, surprised that Nettie should want to tell him something he couldn't guess at.

"Well, my dear?"

"Do you think that we could send our daughter on the Grand Tour as soon as possible?"

"I'm sure I could make arrangements for next month," Dudley conceded, stroking his mustache as best he could. "It would be irregular, Nettie, and it does seem to me that our Leola is a mite too young to go traipsing up and down Europe with some rapscallion guides."

"All the same I think it should be done," Nettie said. "When a white girl starts asking questions about the slaves around her, then it's time overdue to find that white girl as much distraction as possible."

Dudley Stark's eyes widened. "You don't seriously think that our Leola would be the type who—"

"I'm sure not," Nettie said briskly, although she wondered if it ever could be possible to tell who was such a type and who wasn't. "What I think is that something has to be done very quickly, before we have any cause for regret."

"Then you do think she might want to mix? Our Leola?"

"I don't know what to think," Nettie said impatiently. "But send her away from here for a while, and do it as soon as possible. Otherwise, dear, I can't answer for what might happen."

CHAPTER 2

Hannibal didn't get the bad news until the middle of the next afternoon. He was bent over double in order to get at a pesky boll of cotton when a heavy finger pushed at the bottom of his spine.

"I have to talk to you," Rufus said. "It's about your gal, Miriam."

Rufus always managed to find time for doing the things he wanted. He was a fat fellow, had been probably all his life, and he had been at Safe Harbor for as long as he could remember. His daddy had been a house slave to Master Dudley's daddy, and Rufus took advantage of having been at Safe Harbor for such a long time. Master Dudley would get mad at his laziness and call him all sorts of names, but wouldn't sell him. Rufus claimed that he had put some kind of a *juju*, a Voodoo spell, on Master Dudley. Hannibal figured it as being more likely that Master Dudley enjoyed having a fat slave around on the plantation so that he could point to Rufus and tell strangers that he treated all his darkies as well as he treated that one.

"What's wrong?" Hannibal asked when Rufus had led him away from the others.

"Well, that Sarah Jane has done some more damage," Rufus said. "I declare she's a pretty gal, but when she hates it turns out she's good at it."

"If she's hurt Miriam again I'll cut her heart out," Hannibal promised grimly. "What happened?"

"Sarah Jane was helping out your Miriam, like she was

15

supposed to," Rufus said, "but when Mister Joe was looking at them she suddenly turned her back on Miriam and wouldn't do another thing for her. Mister Joe told Miriam to work with both hands, dammit, and not be a lazy nigger gal. Miriam tried, but she couldn't do it. Mister Joe saw what was wrong, for sure. He said the hand could be okay in a few weeks, but Master Dudley wouldn't want a gal just hanging around and eating him outta house and home. He expects she'll be sold."

Hannibal had been ready for that. He made a fist and pounded it against a thigh. "No, she won't be taken away from me. I won't let it happen."

Rufus, at sight of the taller black's hard face, asked, "What are you gonna do?"

"I'm not sure yet, but I'll think on it." Hannibal turned away almost blindly, heading back to the work. "I don't aim to lose her and I won't."

Hannibal had been born a slave, of course, over at Master Jonathan Murtree's plantation. It must have been far away. He didn't remember much about it, except that being a boy had been a lot of fun. The whites would be sent to school while the black boys stayed on the plantation to help pick cotton but generally played games in the fields instead.

The whites were jealous of them for sure, and used to beat up the black boys almost every afternoon when they got back from school. Blacks learned to keep out of the white boys' way except on Saturdays, when the whites would let them alone.

One afternoon that wasn't a Saturday, young Abel Murtree happened to see Hannibal on his way somewhere or other. Hannibal hadn't seen him. Abel suddenly picked up a stick and ran toward Hannibal, screaming, "Black nigger bastard!"

Hannibal did the instinctive thing, whirling around on his tormentor without another thought and striking back.

16

It was a bad mistake. He was severely whipped afterwards and in spite of his mammy's pleading he was sent down the river in chains. Just before he left he found out that Abel Murtree had taken a pretty bad hiding from Master Jonathan for having tried to hurt Hannibal without any reason.

At the slave auction, Hannibal and a number of others stood on a raised wooden platform while older whites prodded and pushed them and counted their teeth and toes. He was a good field hand, and respectful, or so the auctioneer said.

"Too big," one of the slave owners decided. "A buck like that one can grow up so tall that he might make a power of trouble. The best slaves are strong but older. They know that it won't do them no good to make trouble."

Hannibal was put on the block at three auctions before finally being sold at a sacrifice. Otherwise it seemed that Master Simon Grundy would never have bought him.

He was able to do the work of a field slave and he did just that, but it made him so tired at the start that he didn't realize what another slave named Goliath was talking about when he said that a gal named Daisy was making eyes at the new boy.

"Daisy, she makes eyes at everybody," Goliath said, "but she never does nothing more."

"What do you mean?"

"She asked to go with you on church day and sit around with you and what all. You expect you're gonna have a great time, but afterwards she says she don't feel good or she's got a headache or something. Week after week, that gal has headaches."

"Too bad," Hannibal said, taking it for granted that Daisy, whoever she might be, was a sick gal.

Daisy managed to meet him not long afterwards. She turned out to be a big gal, nearly as big as Hannibal him-

17

self. She was pretty, and she bulged a little at the chest. He was fascinated by the shiny tooth in her mouth and she finally said she would show him how it could glow in the dark if he would be with her when it got dark.

They were sitting close to each other on the ground at night, but Daisy didn't open her mouth much. She smiled at him.

"You have to get a lot closer to see the tooth," she said throatily. "A *lot* closer, even than that."

He did. Daisy suddenly gripped him around the shoulders and Hannibal found that he was kissing her. He didn't mind at all. She took his hands and put them on the outside of her breasts through the dress and had him make a circle around the breasts. Finally they stopped the kissing.

"Don't you know what else to do?" she asked, chuckling. "Don't you know what comes next, boy?"

"Yes, but I—" He gulped. "Do you feel all right? You're not sick?"

"For some boys I'm sick," Daisy said carefully. "Whenever they want to go out with me or even if I say I'll go out with 'em and do it, I get sick. Or I say that I got sick. But you ain't one of 'em, Hannibal. It's a fact."

"That's fine," he said with more heartiness than he felt.

"Your first time, isn't it?"

"Of course not," he lied.

Daisy grinned. "Well, your *second* time, then, is gonna be a good one, boy. Come with me."

She led him to a quiet place near the tool shed, where they wouldn't be seen. It seemed as if her clothes were off in a little while, but he was still trying to get his pants down by that time. She had to help him.

"There, that didn't take long." She touched him where it was delicious agony. "My, you're a big fellow, aren't you, Hannibal, honey?"

She lay down first and he lay down next to her. She put his hands where they would excite her, on the breasts.

18

The little red point near the bottom of the breasts started to get hard when she felt his hands.

"Now, Hannibal," she whispered. "Now."

But he didn't know what to do next. She lay down on her back and gestured him to get on top of her. He did, but his weight was too heavy and she groaned. He raised himself a little by using his elbows. Daisy took hold of his big thing again and aimed it so it would be at a very soft spot. Then she put her arms around his behind and pulled as if to force him inside her. He was smiling as he felt his body lower itself and he pressed his tongue against her breast and touched her other breast with the fingers of the nearest hand.

His big thing suddenly got soft. Daisy, who had started to gasp and moan, stopped herself and began jouncing up and down like she was part of something that wasn't really human. It didn't help him at all. Or her. The big thing had gone soft.

She eased him out of her and said, smiling, "Well, there's another way and that's fun, too."

He was on one side again and he felt her lips and tongue on his stomach and his bellybutton and below him on the hair. Then she had taken his big thing and made a fist with it in the center. She put her mouth at the end of it. The big thing got hard again. Her tongue was flicking at the big thing, and then her teeth against as much of it as she had left and that the fist didn't cover. Her teeth pulled at it and she made little noises as if she was holding a straw in water. She kept at that for a while, but it didn't help him.

"Guess you're a rough case, Hannibal," she said after a while. "Are you so scared of me as all that?"

"I'm not," he said stubbornly.

"You think you're not, but that big thing of yours says different." Daisy considered him. "Do you want some advice?"

19

"I don't need—" he started automatically, then cocked his head to listen better.

"Try to take things easier," she smiled. "Don't think you're giving anything away that you can't get back. Make love to a gal because you want to love her and not because you think you ought to."

He blinked. "Is that all?"

"There isn't nothing more that anybody can tell you," Daisy said. "Oh, by the way, if anybody asks you about what happened between us, say that I didn't do nothing for you on account I felt sick. Promise?"

He nodded, but later he couldn't help wondering if everybody who said that Daisy didn't do anything for a man had made her the very same promise after she had come through.

The only other time she asked him to do it with her, it didn't work out, either. But he did find a very nice house slave at the plantation, a gal named Hannah. He liked Hannah, and one thing led to another. Because he remembered Daisy's advice, everything was fine for him when he made love to Hannah.

He was supposed to meet her one night, but a whole bunch of darkies had got away during the day and everybody had to stay in the slave pens when not working. The escaped slaves were brought back a few days afterwards. Twelve of them were hanged one after another, and it was possible to see the bodies sway in the open air next day when they took wagons to the fields in order to do the cotton picking.

The sight was supposed to scare every black boy on the plantation, but it made the others want to get away themselves. Hannibal would have been just the same if he hadn't been tied up with Hannah.

Once a year a new set of clothes would be given to the slaves. Usually they were hand-me-downs from someplace, and getting the new clothes for the year was an event. This time, a few blacks figured that they wouldn't

20

be known in the new clothes and ran away as soon as they had them.

As it happened, Master Simon's overseer got on to what they were trying to do. He used his rifle on a half dozen of the slaves before others got to him and killed him by stamping on his neck when he had fallen to the ground.

The slaves who escaped were never found, but the ones who had killed the overseer were hanged. Master Simon decided to take no more chances on the ungrateful darkies he had bought over the years. He made up his mind to sell them all and buy a new group.

"Won't be worse than any of you," he snarled at them one afternoon in the fields.

Hannibal had often told himself that he'd rather die than go to another slave auction, but he had to go and keep his tongue no matter what was done or said. He was bought by Mister Joe for Dudley Stark of Safe Harbor. Hannibal didn't know it, but Dudley Stark's opinion of slave auctions wasn't much different from his own, and he wouldn't go to one if there was any way to avoid it.

Hannibal didn't have any trouble settling down at Safe Harbor. He made a few friends, made a few enemies, and found a gal for himself on churchgoing day. There was a small house at the back of the slave pens, and on one day a week a circuit-riding preacher would come in for some hallelujah-shouting. He found himself standing next to the gal and they took to each other right away.

Her name was Sarah Jane, and they hit it off for a long time. It was Sarah Jane who introduced him to the short and sweet Miriam, who had just been bought. Sarah Jane wanted Hannibal to help find a boyfriend for her. As soon as she and Hannibal caught sight of each other, Sarah Jane was finished with Hannibal whether she knew it or not.

Hannibal hesitated to quit on her because he didn't want to seem like one of those bucks who are always on the run from one gal to another. But Sarah Jane knew he

21

was colder than he had been and it didn't take long for her to pry the real reason out of Hannibal.

Instead of having him actually walk out on her, she walked out on him. She must have put a million curses on his head and Miriam's, but she walked out and saved as much pride as she could. The way was clear for Hannibal and Miriam. He didn't know when he'd been happier than in those first few weeks with her. They would go together everywhere, lie together and have little jokes all to themselves.

Miriam must have talked a bit too much to some friend of Sarah Jane's, saying that she and Hannibal would be together for keeps and hinting that she'd been able to do the thing that Sarah couldn't do by keeping one man. Sarah Jane had suddenly laced into Miriam yesterday in the fields, and now it did look as if Miriam was going to be sold. But Hannibal had made up his mind that if Miriam left Safe Harbor he would leave, too. He didn't know how, but he was going to be with his Miriam, come hell or high water or both.

CHAPTER 3

Hannibal managed to draw Joe Everdine to one side just after he had counted the blacks in the wagons ready to return from the fields. Joe Everdine was a tall, black-haired man with a hard face and hard hands. He was nearly always dressed in white because he thought that white helped keep the heat down. He was a married man with five kids living off the grounds of Safe Harbor, and he'd have done anything to keep his job. As a result, like most overseers, he did much of the master's dirty work as far as getting the slaves to pick cotton was concerned and keeping them in line when they weren't at work.

"Well, Hannibal?" he began gruffly. "What do you want?"

"Mister Joe, is it true what they say about Master Dudley going to sell my Miriam?"

"Probably. It would take six weeks or so before she can get the use of her arm back, and meanwhile she'll be fed by the auctioneer."

"If you're going to sell Miriam, sell me with her, Mister Joe. Please sell me with her."

"For heaven's sake, why?"

"I want to be with Miriam."

"Hannibal, you've forgotten something," Joe Everdine said. "As lazy niggers go, you're a good worker. I've got no intention whatever of selling a good worker. Neither, of course, has Master Dudley."

"Mister Joe, maybe you don't understand about me and Miriam. We need each other."

23

"Get into the wagon, Hannibal." The overseer turned away. "I don't see enough of my family—that way I can keep feeding them. For all practical purposes, I'm the extra slave at Safe Harbor. We all have to make some sort of sacrifice."

"But there's no fami—"

"*Get into the wagon, Hannibal.*"

With the wagons arrived back at the slave pens, Hannibal strayed from the others. There was a hill just beyond the pens, and he took a deep breath, closed his eyes, stretched out an arm and jumped to the bottom. The hill was no bigger than twenty Hannibals one on top of another, and he didn't hurt himself like he had intended. The arm was still good. He tried it again, but only shook himself up and didn't get hurt.

There was a rock near the bottom of the hill. Hannibal put one arm flat against the earth, but couldn't raise the rock so he might bring it down on the left arm. He decided to try and hit the rock with the arm. That way, he could bust the arm and get sold with Miriam.

"Hannibal!" she called.

He looked up. She was wearing a handkerchief on the broken arm as she stood at the top of the hill and looked down pityingly on him.

He ran to her, embracing her with joy after a moment of staring in wonder, and then kissing her. As ever, her lips were sweet as peaches and her tongue was soft but knew where it wanted to go.

"You mustn't hurt yourself," she said when he had let her go. "I saw you getting away from the others and I want you to promise you won't hurt yourself."

"Then what can I do?"

"You know what we can both do," she said, touching him where it hurt and made him happy at the same time, "now it's so dark."

They lay together on the earth, where they could be

24

hidden from others by a tree. Hannibal didn't know when he had been so happy with a woman. The knowledge that he might not see her again in a short while made him more anxious to please and more delighted that she was with him. It took time together, but not enough time.

Afterwards, when they were in each other's arms, Hannibal said, "Guess you'll be going tomorrow."

"That'll be Sunday, churchgoing day." Miriam smiled. "Master Dudley wouldn't send me away on the Lord's day, even if it means having to feed me that much extra."

"The day after church day will be it, then."

"Hannibal, will you do something if I ask you?"

"Sure I will. What?"

Miriam said softly, "Marry me."

Hannibal blinked, then looked carefully at her. "It won't do any good, even if Mister Joe would let us—or would it?"

"Sure it would."

"If Mister Joe knows we want to stay together so much, he might ask Master Dudley to keep us together," Hannibal said stubbornly. "Mister Joe is hard, but he's fair. I know it."

"If you think anything good about him, Hannibal, then you think what I don't." She stared. "Where are you off to?"

"Have to find Mister Joe before he goes away for church day."

He found Joe Everdine in front of his trap and gathering the reins. Joe Everdine wore a white cloth cap and square-rimmed glasses.

"Hannibal, for heaven's sake, I'm going home for as much rest as a man with five squalling brats can possible get," Joe Everdine said. "It can't be so important that you have to stop me now, I'm sure."

"Mister Joe, can me and Miriam get married?"

"Can you—what?" He whirled, giving Hannibal his

25

full attention now. "A pair of slaves wanting to *marry?*"

Hannibal said sullenly, "Ben and Martha have got married up, Mister Joe."

"Those two have been together forever, and nobody could imagine them apart."

"Well, me and Miriam don't want nothing much more than being together and—"

"Listen, Hannibal, you and this gal are going to be away from each other in a couple of days, and you'll almost certainly never see her again. Marriage isn't a gift that you give some woman, but it's something that is supposed to work for every day of the week. I'm almost tempted to tell you—well, never mind that. There are certain facts of living that no slave would believe for a moment."

"Mister Joe, can't me and Miriam—?"

"No, I'm not able to do anything that might hurt my job," Joe Everdine said. "I can't keep a nigger gal at Safe Harbor for six weeks when she isn't able to work."

"Mister Joe, I'll do her work, too, if you'll just keep her on. I swear I will."

"I'm sorry, Hannibal, but I can't take the chance." Joe Everdine shook his head. "You only think you love this gal and nobody else, Hannibal, but there are plenty of watermelons in the patch, believe me."

Hannibal turned away, eyes cast down.

Joe Everdine said kindly, "If you were white and free, Hannibal, you'd know the big secret of the ages. The secret that married people have been keeping from others since a little bit after the first marriage. Do you know what that secret really is? Do you *want* to know what that secret really is? How would you like to find out for yourself and be the only unmarried person who really knows it? Okay? Then I'll tell you the one thing that all married people know and that those who aren't hitched up will never believe. You won't believe it, either, but at

26

least you'll be getting a chance that single people never get." ·

And he looked around to make sure nobody could see him or hear him except for Hannibal.

Then he leaned forward and whispered, "No marriage whatever is really worth a damn!"

"Mister Joe!" Hannibal was shocked.

"It's true, boy. Why would you marry? For love? A big buck like you can get that from any nigger gal at Safe Harbor. You think that if you marry you won't want to roam? Your eye gets sharper as you get older, Hannibal, and your wife rubs your nose in it by pointing out all the pretty girls as you walk the street, as if to tell you what a fool you were for having got married in the first place and how helpless you are to do anything about it. A woman can never forgive a man for having had such low taste as to marry *her*. Besides, all women are bone-mean, Hannibal. It comes with the franchise, believe me."

Hannibal didn't know what Mister Joe was talking about and didn't know if he was supposed to nod or smile or what.

"Would you marry for money? You haven't got a chance of that, and if you could do it your wife would always be reminding you that you had only got married for money. What about saving money? A wife adds to expenses, buying the foolishest things you can imagine. For friendship? A wife's interests are different from yours after a while and she sits around at breakfast and tells you the price of every store-bought item of food you're eating. And you should never marry for young 'uns. They scream and scream when they're new and they get pretty damn ungrateful when they grow up. The more I chew on it, Hannibal, the more convinced I become that a man and his wife have got nothing whatsoever in common."

"My Miriam wouldn't never do things like that."

"She's a woman, isn't she?" Mister Joe slapped the

27

reins on the horses' backs. "I'm doing you a favor, Hannibal, believe me. Stay away from marriage—I declare, these horses must have some nigra blood in 'em, they're so lazy. Get *on!*"

Mister Joe drove off finally, but slowly. Hannibal looked after him as if wanting to run and catch up and talk some more, but then he turned and nearly ran back to the tree where Miriam was waiting for him.

"I know what happened," Miriam said softly. "It's on your face. I can't read, but I know how to read your face real good, Hannibal."

"Miriam, I can't take much more of this," he said softly. "I'm trying the best I know how, but I have my borders and this has gone past them. I want to marry you and I'm gonna do it, Miriam. I want to be with you and I'm gonna do that, too, no matter what they say."

Miriam said quietly, "We can get married tomorrow, if you want that."

Hannibal stared at her. "After the church, you mean?"

"Yes."

"It might be the one chance we'll ever have, I s'pose," he agreed. "I'll talk to Brother Alfred before the hallelujah-shouting gets started up."

The slaves of Safe Harbor were walking into the shack that was used as a church, doing it slowly and carefully as if they didn't want to lose more calm fresh air than they had to, and were glad they could come late to something.

Brother Alfred stood on the raised platform, shuffling papers with writing on them, watching the congregation come in. He was a tall, clean-shaven man who carried a book with him everywhere as if he wanted to show white folks that he was able to read. Not a day went by that he wasn't preaching somewhere or other, and he generally kept to the Old Testament stories and the spiritual singing that followed. His congregations didn't like to hear anything from the New Testament; some of them said that the sufferings of Jesus Christ couldn't have amounted to so much because Christ wasn't a slave. Brother Alfred had found, though, that he could retell the story of the Hebrews being freed from bondage week after week if he wanted to, even though none of his congregants was really clear what a Hebrew was.

Hannibal asked Brother Alfred to step to one side, which the cleric did. Brother Alfred glanced from the huge Hannibal to the shy girl at his side.

"Miriam, aren't you?" Brother Alfred smiled at her, then turned. "I don't remember as I've seen you among the worshipers before this, brother."

"I've been here." Hannibal didn't say that he came to church maybe one time in five or six. "I want to get married to this gal. To Miriam."

"Congratulations." Brother Alfred beamed. " 'Whoso findeth a wife findeth a treasure.' That's from the Song of Solomon, and considering how many wives he had, you got to admit he was in a position to know. Can I see your permissions, please?"

"Our what?" Hannibal blinked.

"I got to have your master's permission in writing for you two to marry," Brother Alfred said. "Otherwise I can't do nothing."

Miriam asked quietly, "Just this time, can't you do it without?"

"Oh I could do it, sister, but when the whites find out I won't be allowed to come and preach here any more. Or anyplace else, for all I know. I heard of one nigger preacher who got himself tarred and feathered, and no incident like that is going to happen to Brother Alfred."

"Thanks very much," Hannibal said bitterly.

Brother Alfred waggled his head. "If you want to do the first thing as strikes your fancy, boy, you have to buy yourself free beforehand."

"With what?" Hannibal demanded loudly "Don't you think I'd do that if it was possible?"

"Not so loud," Brother Alfred said "You're disturbing the others."

"They're no good, either." Hannibal whirled, facing the other slaves on their wooden benches Cords stood out on his neck, swelling with anger. "Do you hear what I say? You're just a bunch of nigger fools, the whole lot of you, and what you get is just what you deserve "

He hurried out of that place, not knowing or caring just then if Miriam was with him. When he got outside, having nearly crashed the door down, she spoke to him with quiet despair.

"Hannibal, there's nothing the likes of us can possibly go out and do."

He turned to face her, his mind made up without his ever having thought of it. At no time had he said to himself what would have to be done, but as soon as the words came out he knew he was right and he ought to have tried it a long time ago.

"This much we can do for a start," he said. "Get away from Safe Harbor."

Miriam drew a dusky hand up to her neck. "Escape, you mean?"

He nodded.

"But we can't. When we're brought back, there isn't any way of knowing what might happen to us except that it'll be real bad."

"It's that or nothing," Hannibal said roughly. "Let's not talk about it over here. If we're the only two who know, the better it is for us."

But a third voice suddenly said, "Well, I know it, too, now, and if you need any help you just have to tell me."

It was Rufus, the fat slave, who had waddled out of the shack used for church. He stood grinning from Miriam to Hannibal and back again, gazing his fill at her.

"Let's all three of us have a little talk in private, over

30

there," Rufus said, pointing to a shady spot where they could see if anybody came close. "I can't stand all that whining in church and this here escape of yours ought to be a lot more fun to talk about, if you ask me."

On Sunday in the late afternoon, Joe Everdine and his wife and one or two of their five children would generally ride over to Safe Harbor and have tea with the Starks. They agreed between themselves beforehand that they'd stay no more than an hour and on the way back they generally talked about how they had behaved in front of the Starks, as often as not ending with an argument of the sort that made Joe happy to get back to work on Monday morning. At the very least, the talk gave Dudley a chance to hear anything he might have missed during the week about the work of cotton picking at Safe Harbor.

On this Sunday there was another couple as guests, the Everdines discovered, and they wondered if their own presence had been wanted. Nettie Stark, regretting to herself that she had forgotten to let Joe Everdine know that she and Dudley would be occupied this Sunday, made a point of putting the Everdines at ease. Mrs. Everdine was a slim, small creature with wide staring eyes, and she was grateful for every favor.

The guests were Andrew Hollis and his wife. Andrew Hollis was a plantation owner twenty miles east of Safe Harbor. He and his wife had come to the Starks for a sociable Sunday afternoon following church.

While the ladies chatted in the far corner of the parlor, all except Leola Stark, who was looking across a bit wistfully at her father and male guests, Dudley crossed his legs and turned to the visitor.

"What in tunket, Andrew, are we going to do about this slavery investigation, so-called, by those fools in Washington?"

Andrew Hollis pursed his lips. "A few of us have got

31

together to launch a heavy campaign of letter-writing to legislators. And we've sent a representative down to Washington to argue against an investigation. We've hired Cyrus Follansbee to lead our campaign, and he's very skillful at turning the legislators around when that needs to be done. He gives the impression that he's only talking about the facts of a matter, but his facts are heavily loaded for the side which has hired him."

"Met him once." Dudley frowned. "He likes men more than women, I should think."

From Leola there came a gasp of pleasurable horror. Dudley glared at her and she made a point of looking at the other women until a glance at the mirror told her that her father's attention was riveted to his guest again.

Andrew Hollis was saying quietly, "We'll get our way again in Washington, Dudley. We always do."

Dudley grumbled, "I wish I had been informed about these steps when they were decided on."

Andrew Hollis reached for his snuffbox, dipped some snuff between thumb and forefinger, drew the fingers to one nostril, withdrew the fingers, and sneezed cheerfully. "A number of the boys who don't know you as well as they ought to, Dudley, felt that your temper might make you a disruptive influence."

There was a pause while Dudley Stark decided against shouting that he didn't have any temper at all, goddammit.

Joe Everdine stepped into the pause. "If those people in Washington knew the darkies as well as we do, there wouldn't be any investigation at all. Take away slavery from the darkie and he has got nothing."

Joe suddenly remembered having spoken for a few moments to Sarah Jane just before coming up to the house. Sarah Jane had been bitter and jealous, and she had talked against the slave who was called Hannibal.

"Why, Mr. Stark, you provide church facilities for them, you know, as a good Christian master should, and

32

you'd think that Negroes wouldn't abuse those. But they certainly do. Only this morning, one of them suddenly stood up and began shouting at the other nigras and saying that they're no good and worthless and whatall. Who else but a nigra would foul up a church in that way?"

The others agreed. Leola, who had been listening again, suddenly felt like standing up and telling the men that they were a trio of fools.

For it stood to reason that only one slave would have done such a thing so boldly, only one. It was the big handsome black she had seen a few days ago, the one who she had later been told was named Rufus. She knew it had to be him and that he hated being at Safe Harbor as much as she did and that nobody else felt the same way about it. More than anything she wanted to talk it over with this slave, this Rufus. She wanted to hear what he had to say, this fellow creature who had been pushed to a point of no return.

She stood up suddenly and turned to the women. "Excuse me, mother, ladies," she said, and turned to the door. Back of her, Andrew Hollis sneezed again on account of another dose of snuff.

Leola was going to the slave pens to see this black man, this Rufus, to be with him for only a little while and talk about their mutual hatred of Safe Harbor. All that she'd to would be to talk to the handsome black. Nothing else would happen between them. Of course not.

CHAPTER 4

The slave pens occupied four rundown shacks set
against the far end of the plantation. There was a patch of
garden behind it, which the slaves could use to grow simple foods for themselves, but they were generally so tired
from field work that the garden was rundown, too. There
was a bad smell in the air close to the slave pens, and it
made a well-bred girl want to stuff her nostrils.

Leola dismounted from Buttercup, having taken the
trouble to ride sidesaddle out to the pens. She walked at
the horse's side, hoping that the familiar horse smells
would drive the bad slave pen smells from her consciousness.

Three slaves who had been lolling around in front of
the pens suddenly stood up, fear written on all their faces.
Leola advanced, smiling.

"No need to get worried, boys," she said quickly to
put them at their ease. "I only want to talk to a slave called
Rufus. Where is he?"

"Asleep, Miss Leola, if I know that rascal," one of the
boys said. Another one started to laugh, but cut himself
short.

"Please send him out to me," Leola said. "I'll be waiting over there."

She gestured a little distance away, near a patch of
greenery and some trees that ought to drive the slave
pens smell away. They didn't do it entirely, she found
out when she reached the haven. There was a curious

noise nearby, almost as if somebody was talking but not quite that.

One of the shack doors opened and an enormous fat man waddled out. On his face, too, fear was written.

Leola, watching him, instantly knew that her father had named the wrong slave. As he waddled forward, hand near his face as if to ward off any blows, Leola shook her head impatiently.

"I'm not going to hurt you," she said, although she couldn't blame him for thinking so if her face had suddenly reflected her thoughts.

"Y-yes, miss," Rufus agreed, bringing the smell nearer to her as he walked.

"Please stand where you are," she said, and wondered why the nearby murmuring she'd listened to only a moment before had suddenly come to a stop. "Your name is Rufus, I suppose."

"Yes, Miss Leola." There was hunger on the black face, and something that made her skin crawl even though she couldn't tell what the emotion might be.

"I was looking for another slave," she said. "This one is tall and very black and muscular. I know that's an unusual discription for a slave and I want you to tell me who he is."

" 'Who he is'?"

"I want to know his name and I want to talk to him."

"Right now?"

"Yes, of course."

Rufus had glanced sharply into the trees, but then he turned away and began to scratch his head. He tried to look as if he was thinking, but his eyes on her were sharp.

"Miss Leola," he drawled, "I don't rightly know what you mean by that word muss-kew-lar."

Leola had carried a riding crop with her and now she made a point of raising the hand in which she carried it. The slave drew back, terified.

"Miss Leola, if I knew where to find the boy you want,

35

I sure would tell you, Miss Leola." He added, in a different voice, "Never was I so close to a white gal before. Never."

"Maybe you don't know where he is—I say, maybe," she admitted. "But you know who he is. Tell me his name."

"His name?" Another sharp look through the trees, or so it seemed, and then back to her.

"He's the only strong one at Safe Harbor and all I have to do is ask Joe Everdine and I'll get the name right away. Well, Rufus?"

"His name? Oh yes, Miss Leola, it's—uh, I'm not sure I can recollect—"

She said quickly, "Good day, Rufus. I'll see you again, you can be sure."

She started Buttercup around and toward the trees. Behind her, Rufus' voice was high-pitched and keening, a wail of misery.

"It's Hannibal, Miss Leola. The boy you want, his name is Hannibal." He shouted, "Hannibal! Lord forgive me, Hannibal!"

Leola turned briefly in the saddle, and rode off. The murmuring sounds she'd heard before had stopped completely, but on the horse she was able to move faster than anybody on foot. She didn't generally like to use the riding whip, but this time she spurred Buttercup on.

The black was bent over almost double at a point behind a gnarled tree. Swiftly she took in the sight of him, saw the bulge of muscles on the arms and in the thick legs. Her heart set up a pounding that she felt could be heard from the earth below.

"You!" she called. "Boy!"

He straightened up. For the first time these two were face to face.

The man she saw was even more handsome than she had imagined from a distance. The blackness added to his looks. The play of muscles in his arms and the glint

36

of sun across his shoulders made him, to her, almost un-bearably handsome.

As for Hannibal, he had never in life been this close to a white woman, a blonde white woman, and he gazed as if he hadn't really seen a woman before. He loved and wanted Miriam; he had sent her away only a little while ago to fetch more food for the two of them on their escape trip; but he suddenly wanted this white girl with all his heart and soul.

Leola knew the answer to the question she now asked. "Your name is Hannibal?"

He nodded.

"Why are you over here. of all places? You should be over at the slave pens."

He said nothing.

Leola didn't have the slightest idea what to say next. There were any number of things she wanted to tell him in looking for a common ground with this slave, but nothing was said. It occurred to her only too late that a girl didn't spend social time with one of her father's slaves.

"I still don't know what you're doing out here," she said if only to hear herself talking, "unless you're making plans to escape or you're already going to—"

She stopped herself. One look at his thrusting jaw had told her the truth. He stepped forward, as if he was going to keep her from leaving. Leola tightened her grip on the riding crop, but didn't raise it.

"You're getting away from here," she said, and her feelings of envy were almost too much for her. "I wish I could go, too."

Hannibal drew back and looked at her eyes for the first time. "You? Why, you can go when you want."

He might just as well have said to her that there was no reason in the world for any white-skinned person to be unhappy.

"I can't go when I want," she said sullenly. "I'm just as much a slave as anybody else at Safe Harbor."

"If you run out you won't have to kiss the rope when somebody brings you back."

"There's more to slavery than just being in chains."

"If you're a real slave, chains are enough." Hannibal paused. "What do you want here?"

She said, "Tell me where you're going so I can go, too."

"This is crazy talk!"

"No, it's not and I'll prove it. I'll go with you."

Hannibal said mechanically, "Now I know you're crazy."

"I'm not." She was exultant. "You want to get away and I can help you. If we're together on the road, then you're the slave and I'm the mistress."

She knew perfectly well that the word "mistress" could take two meanings, and paused after she had said it.

"There won't be any questions asked," she added. "We can get away."

Hannibal looked down. There was considerable truth to the things she said, of course; but that wasn't enough to explain what was happening.

"What makes you want to do this?" he asked.

"Adventure, or maybe I want to help somebody for once in my life." Leola shrugged. "Don't ask questions. It's sure to kill things if you ask questions."

"Let me think," he said swiftly. "This is all happening so fast I can't think."

She didn't know just what made it happen as it did, and probably she never would know. But she descended from the horse and walked closer to Hannibal, perhaps wanting to comfort him. There was no odor on him except a light sweat. He stood with legs apart, staring at her without being able to move.

Leola's heart was pounding so furiously she felt sure it would burst through her skin. She was walking rigidly, like a doll that had just been wound up. Her hands were outstretched, one hand with the riding whip in it; and her feet were wide apart.

38

She didn't see the small stone that tripped her, but even as she was falling she knew a moment's gratitude that the incident was happening. She had fallen at the feet of the imposing black giant who now towered above her.

She never knew why she did the next thing so mechanically or why the raving hunger for him seemed to take over her very soul. All she actually knew was that she leaned forward and opened his pants buttons at the middle and drew out his sex, already rigid. Then she put her free hand around him, spreading the fingers over one firm male buttock. She leaned forward.

From above the black man gasped, and then his hands touched her cheeks lightly. One hand suddenly went to the back of her neck as if to bring her closer.

Only a short while passed in ecstasy for her before it happened. There was a gasp from him, the infusion of sticky warmth, and without letting go she tried to make it happen to him once more.

And back of her, sounds could be heard coming towards them. He must have heard the sounds first. His thumbs suddenly prodded the sides of her jaws, forcing her mouth open.

Dazed and hurt by the sounds, it seemed, Leola whirled around. She was on her knees, her lips were moist and sticky, and she knew that the black man's sex was still in sight.

A black girl came swiftly into the clearing. In one hand she carried a pair of food packages; her other arm was in a black sling. She was small and fairly attractive for a colored girl, if a man cared for that type.

She saw the guilt on the faces of Hannibal and Leola, and she called out with shock.

In Leola's mind there was only one thought: the black gal must never tell what she had seen.

Swiftly she rose, riding whip held firmly in her hand. The black gal had been coming toward them, but she suddenly stopped. She didn't move forward any longer, but she didn't run for her life, either. She might very well have been hypnotized.

Hannibal was shouting, "Run from here, gal! Whatever you do, run!"

The horse, Buttercup, sensing the tension, began to neigh in near-hysteria.

There was no time for the black girl to run, though, not any more. Leola raised the riding crop and brought it down flush across the girl's eyes. The girl screamed at the agony of pain that had come upon her.

Every noise seemed to happen at once: the girl screaming, Hannibal shouting, the horse neighing; and the crack of the whip.

Swiftly, Leola brought the whip down across the girl's breast, full-strength. Her scream stopped all of a sudden, with breath-catching quickness.

Even as the girl fell forward, Leola heard from her daze that every other sound had stopped at the same time. Buttercup was pawing the ground now, and that was the only sound at all in the clearing.

Hannibal, breaking the training of a lifetime, had come toward the white girl with intentions to stop her, but he could do nothing useful any longer. It had taken so much time before he could make himself try to stop the white girl that it had cost the life of the woman he had loved.

Leola turned to Hannibal, the riding whip brandished in air. Near-hysteria of her own had changed her from the girl who had wanted to help him run away.

"If you tell one word about what happened between us, you'll die," she snapped, her voice changed out of recognition. "That's a promise. Now get out of Safe Harbor. Get out, get out, and be thankful I won't stop you."

She was sobbing as she mounted Buttercup sidesaddle and the horse hooves sounded like a tattoo of rifle shots as she rode back to the stable.

Hannibal stayed in place for a moment. In return for

his silence he was to be given the chance to get away. He wouldn't let his mind rest on the things that had just happened. He looked down instead at the dead body of Miriam, lying on her face. There was a leaf beside her. He reached for it and tore the green off so that only the spine was left. He made a circle of the spine and tied a knot in it. With that, he approached the dead body.

He didn't know which hand to put the just-made ring on; as it happened he used the right hand because it was closest to him. He didn't know which finger a ring belonged on, either, so he put it on the first finger.

"I wed you, gal," he said softly. "I wed you."

He couldn't bear to look at her face and since she was on her stomach he simply leaned over and kissed the back of her head.

Then he stood up, took the food packages from her and started to run. Instinct alone told him that he was away from Safe Harbor at last. Instead of slackening his pace, Hannibal ran more quickly. He had escaped, but he wasn't free. Not yet.

PART TWO

CHAPTER 5

Dudley had sent the Everdines home and was bidding goodbye to Andrew and Samantha Hollis. The last he saw of Andrew, his fellow plantation owner was reaching for that invaluable snuffbox of his, and Samantha was sighing resignedly. The inevitable sneeze might very well have made the horses more active, like a whipcrack over their heads. They moved before the driver was ready, putting him off-balance for a moment.

Dudley started back to the plantation, vaguely annoyed because Nettie hadn't come out with him to say *au revoir* to the guests. Nettie had been waylaid by one of the house slaves and had excused herself and hurried away.

Now it was Nettie who met him at the door as he came to it. Fresh lines had appeared on her forehead, and Dudley hoped they'd go away soon. She looked exactly the way Dudley remembered her mother as having looked.

"What's wrong now?" he started.

"Something serious has happened to Leola," Nettie said promptly. "She's upstairs and crying fit to die."

"Well, I suppose it's an attack of the vapors," Dudley said. Young girls were always having the vapors, it seemed, and so were old maids.

"Vapors, my foot!" Nettie said vigorously. "I've sent

42

one of the boys for Dr. Simmons. Whatever this is, believe me it's nothing to make fun of."

"Nonsense. She was fine only an hour ago. I'll talk her out of this, myself."

Against Nettie's advice he went up to his daughter's room. Leola lay on the bed amidst pale pink decorations, sobbing bitterly, but no tears now ran from her eyes. Tears had already stained and discolored her face and no more were left.

"Don't you worry," her father said comfortingly. "Next month you'll be going on the Grand Tour of Europe. Sooner than you had expected, baby, isn't it? Your ma and me have been talking it over and we've decided it's time for you to go."

Leola stared at him, transfixed. At any other occasion she would have burst out laughing. She had ached to go on the Grand Tour as soon as possible, but now she only wanted to stay at Safe Harbor, at home.

If nothing else she wanted to know whether or not Hannibal would get away. She would have gone with him if the colored gal hadn't interfered and would have been with him now. The trouble had unsettled her so much when it happened that she hadn't been able to think straight and had only wanted to return to her folks.

"Don't worry, sweetheart," Dudley said, and touched her hand comfortingly. She withdrew it so swiftly that he was stunned. For a moment she seemed to be on the point of screaming.

Dudley Stark was uneasy when he returned to the parlor where his wife waited. Nettie was staring down at a riding crop that had been set down across one of the inlaid marquetry tables. It was wet.

"Moses brought that to me from the stable," she said. "It's Leola's."

"What about—?" A closer look showed him that it was covered with blood. "I won't have her whipping a horse like that."

43

"Not a horse," Nettie said. "Moses told me that, for a fact. He looked very reproachfully at me, too, when he said it."

"Has our Leola been at one of the slaves?" Dudley frowned. "She'd better have a damned good reason for it. I'm not going to have a slave damaged like that unless there's—"

One of the girl house slaves came into the parlor. Her face was solemn, her eyes downcast.

"Pardon, Master Dudley, but one of the boys is asking to see you out the back way. He says it's very serious."

Dudley started out, but stopped as a house slave ushered in Dr. Simmons. The doctor was a pompous man with curly mustaches and middle-long sideburns. He carried a black leather medical bag. Nettie walked with him up to Leola's room, telling what had happened, with an unconscious emphasis on her own, Nettie's, reactions.

"I've never seen her like this . . . I was stunned, doctor, absolutely stunned . . ."

Dudley told the house slave that he'd see the field boy outside, but in a little while.

Nettie joined him again shortly afterwards and the two of them waited for Simmons to return. For once Nettie was so upset that she couldn't even talk about household matters. She kept busy with needlework, which quieted her nerves. Dudley had been forbidden to smoke cigars in the parlor, so he punched his fists against his knees.

Simmons appeared in ten minutes by Dudley's pocket watch. His face was grave, but he didn't sound as if the news would be very bad.

"Your daughter has no physical illness, I'm glad to say," Dr. Simmons began, "but she's under a severe strain which she won't talk about."

Nettie asked, "What can we do to make her feel better?"

44

Doctor Simmons sat down to write a prescription. "You'll send one of the boys for this, and if you've got any of that sedative I prescribed for you a few months back, Mrs. Stark, I suggest giving it to her in the meantime."

"I hate to give my child any medicine with laudanum in it," Nettie said, "but you're the doctor, of course."

Dudley said, "I take it that you don't know what brought on this nervous state of my daughter's."

"No idea. Why, she didn't even want me to touch her and I'm the one who brought her into the world in the first place. But when I touched her she started to shout. I'm a little surprised that all of Alabama didn't hear it."

"Thank you very much, doctor," Dudley said. "I'll walk to the carriage with you."

On the way, he saw one of the field slaves waiting in the clearing. The slave twisted a straw hat around in his hands. He was in a state of considerable agitation.

After shaking the doctor's hand and saying that he would pay when he received a proper bill, Dudley walked across the field toward where the barefoot slave waited. Halfway there he stopped himself and gestured for the slave to come to him. The slave was a five-footer named Hiram, who picked cotton with the best of them.

"Is anything wrong, Hiram?" Dudley Stark asked. "Are some of the other boys giving you trouble because you work too fast?"

Hiram had been beaten up twice by some of the other boys because he simply didn't like to work slowly. He seemed to have learned his lesson, but still worked a bit quicker and more carefully than most of the others.

"Not this time, Master Dudley," the slave said. "It's about Miriam."

Dudley remembered all his slaves. Miriam was the short and perky gal who had broken her arm not long ago. She was the type he'd have rolled in the hay if she had been white and willing, but even in his younger days

45

when his friends had been coupling with slave gals he had refused to have anything to do with them in that way. He tried to treat his slaves as well as anybody else did, but he simply found the color repulsive to touch. One of his big arguments with Nettie had been that he had wanted to hire a white cook and not have to feel that some Negro had been touching his food, but Nettie wouldn't hear of it and he had lost his case.

"Is Miriam all right?" he asked. "If she isn't, what's wrong with her?"

"She's dead, master," Hiram said sadly. "Somebody whipped her to death."

Dudley closed his eyes tightly, remembering the riding crop with its bloodstains.

"Do you have any idea who did it?"

"No, master, but we do have to bury her."

Dudley nodded. In Alabama weather, a corpse couldn't be left above ground for long.

"Master Dudley, I'll tell the boys to start digging in the slave cemetery. And I hope it will be all right if Brother Alfred goes to the slave cemetery on Sunday and says a few words over her."

"Of course, Hiram."

Dudley hurried back into the parlor, where Nettie had been waiting. He fumed, opening and shutting his fists in bad temper.

"Do you know what your daughter did? She whipped a gal slave to death."

Nettie flinched. "I don't believe it."

"You will." Swiftly he repeated Hiram's story. "I'm going up to her room and have it out with her. If she wants to destroy valuable property, I plan to find out the reason why."

"Dear, she's not well."

"She'll be even sicker when I get finished with her," Dudley vowed.

46

Nettie went with him, of course. They found Leola staring with sightless eyes at the ceiling.

"Why did you whip that gal?" Dudley began without preamble. He was standing near the head of her bed, a forefinger extended threateningly. "You'd better have a reason and it better be good or I swear I'll take a riding crop to you myself."

Leola started to put a hand over her mouth. Dudley took the hand instead, pulled it down on the bed and put some pressure on it.

"Don't try any flummery with me," Dudley said carefully. "I don't want to hear that you feel bad or that I'm a beast or even that you want to do yourself some harm. None of those things interest me. All I want to know is why you whipped that slave gal to death. All I want you to do is tell me what happened."

"Why—nothing." She was agitated, though, and she flicked at her blonde hair with a shaky hand.

"So you whipped a nigger gal to death but nothing happened. Is that right?"

"I didn't do anything."

"There's blood on your riding crop and a nigger gal has been whipped to death—"

"Must you say those same words all the time?"

"Yes."

Leola drew a deep breath. "Daddy, you'll only be sorry if I tell you what happened."

Nettie had been looking tautly from father to daughter. She had started by looking anxiously at Leola, as if to make sure her health could stand under the pressure of her father's questioning. For the first time she gave her daughter a disapproving look.

"If you say a thing like that," Nettie pointed out slowly, "you can be sure that your daddy is going to get everything out of you. Your daddy and I."

Leola looked down. Tears traveled down her cheeks.

47

Nettie said, "I think that Leola is trying to decide exactly what she'll tell and what she'll leave out. I've seen that sort of look on her before when that's what she was doing."

Dudley said remorselessly, "If I haven't heard from you before I count to five, I'm going to give you the worst damn shaking you ever had."

At any other time Leola would have smiled; everybody in the room knew that Dudley Stark would rather cut out his tongue than put a hand in anger to his daughter. Nettie moved closer to the bed, perhaps to put the threat into action when Dudley found that he couldn't do it. The last few moments had changed Nettie's attitude toward Leola's illness.

"One," he began, "two . . . three . . . I'm warning you, gal . . . four . . ."

"Wait, Daddy." Leola rolled her eyes briefly. "I went riding, as you probably know. I wanted to work off some of my extra energy and distract myself. Buttercup took me toward the slave quarters. I tried to steer her away, but I couldn't."

Nettie asked sharply, "Are you saying that you have no control over the gentlest filly that God ever made?"

"I'm saying that I didn't have any control this time."

"Go on. I want to hear more of this," Dudly said, his breath coming evenly. "What happened?"

"This slave suddenly appeared. A great hulking brute. He reached up and held me, forcing me off Buttercup and forcing me to drop the reins or choke the filly. Then he dropped me to the earth and he lay down beside me and—oh, Daddy, it was terrible."

Dudley Stark's face had changed from the normal pink-white to an angry red.

"Are you saying what I think you're saying, gal?"

"Daddy, he forced my clothes off and he—he climbed on top of me. Oh, it was horrible, daddy, it was horrible! It was disgusting and vile."

Nettie said quietly, almost coolly, "You do realize, don't you, that for all practical purposes you have just condemned another slave to death?"

And Dudley said quietly, "I'll kill him. I swear by God Almighty I'll kill that black bastard."

"Mother, I'm telling the truth! That's what happened."

"If that's the case, I would think you'd have whipped the buck to death and not the nigger gal."

"I'll kill him," Dudley said again. "I swear I'll whip him to death with my own hands."

Leola stared at her mother, but said nothing.

Nettie asked, "Well, what about the girl you killed? Tell me about her."

"She was just a piece of property, that's all," Leola said sullenly. "You don't have to take on about it."

"Tell me and your father how it happened."

Leola paused long enough to take a deep breath and then said, "When it was finally over, thank the Lord, and he grinned at me in that disgusting way, I heard a gal chuckling. Then she started calling things out to me."

Dudley, making fists and letting them go, said quietly, "If that's what she did, she deserved everything she got and a little extra besides."

" 'If,' " Nettie said levelly, "is a big word."

Dudley looked at his daughter. "What happened after that, dear? You don't have to be afraid to tell us."

"Well, I was so angry at her for what she'd said that I pulled myself up and reached for the riding crop. All I wanted to do at first was to hit her across the eyes because those eyes had seen what happened between me and— I mean, what he, that man slave, had done to me."

"And what happened afterwards?"

"I must have put my clothes on, somehow. That black devil was gone. I ran and ran. Buttercup had run away, but I saw her circling the general area. I called her and she stopped. I don't know how I managed to get on her, but I did. She took me back to the stables, almost as if she knew I was at the end of my wits. I must have staggered back to the house."

Nettie said, "Some of the things you say are in a different tone of voice from the others. When you talk about why you hit that gal across the eyes and about the horse taking you back to the stables, you're relaxed and remembering something. When you talk about the slave tearing off your clothes and being taken advantage of, Leola, your voice is slow and hesitant. It's as if you're trying to decide exactly which words to use."

Dudley Stark suddenly whirled around. "I'll kill Hannibal. I swear I will. It couldn't have been anybody else."

Nettie said gently, "Before you can occupy yourself like that, dear, there's one other matter to take care of."

"Nothing is more important than this."

"It concerns your daughter's welfare."

Dudley, halfway to the door, scowled as he turned to look at his wife.

Nettie explained, "Dr. Simmons did not know what our daughter says happened to her. Now that there is more knowledge to go on, a further examination will be needed. I can only hope it will not be too painful for Leola."

"You mean in case there's a—a child on the way? A pickaninny? God!"

Dudley Stark, galvanized, ran out of the room to find the nearest house slave and order him to fetch the doctor. Nettie, staying behind in the doorway, turned to Leola. There was no pity or compassion on her face.

"I can guess what really happened between you and that black buck," she said coolly. "I could overlook that, but I can't overlook your sending him to his death now that he has satisfied you in your shameful act."

"Mother, you don't understand!"

"I may not know some of the details," Nettie admitted,

"but don't try to tell me that you're just an innocent child. You weren't even born innocent."

Leola said, "If you're so convinced of that, why are you telling Daddy to bring Dr. Simmons back?"

"Because, my child, if you're putting a fellow human being to death, you should be made to suffer some inconvenience for it, at least."

Downstairs, Dudley was shouting. Nettie closed the door on her daughter and hurried to the winding, curved, carpeted stairs.

Leola listened to her mother's footsteps for as long as she could hear them, then sighed. Her mother was far from being a fool. Not that Daddy was a fool either, but he was so fond of his daughter that he could be blinded.

She had done the only thing she could possibly do by putting the blame on Hannibal. He must have been free and away from Safe Harbor by now, but if he wasn't she could certainly not dream of letting him ever tell anybody who knew her, white or black, what had happened in that clearing.

Leola knew enough of the "facts of life" to be sure that she would be examined by Dr. Simmons to see if she was a virgin or not.

In her anxiety she remembered, from out of the recent past, having heard some girl refer to a boy as "not having any wick in his candle." She had understood what the girl meant, but at the time had made believe she didn't.

There were a number of candles in the upper drawer of her bureau. Leola tiptoed out of bed and opened the drawer as silently as she could manage, in spite of squeaks from the bureau and creaks from the floor. She drew out two candles of different widths, held the first one against her body, then spread her legs and lowered the candle. She pressed the candle against herself, but without success. She put that candle back.

With the second candle she repeated the process. There

51

was a pause. She winced and had to clamp her lips tight to keep from calling out. She pushed the candle more deeply into herself. It was hard to know at what point to stop so that her body would look to a doctor as if it had been violated. She decided to push the candle in as deep as it would go, still holding the far end.

By the time she drew it out her face was pale and she barely had enough energy to put the candle back into the drawer and stagger back to bed. From being ill at a recent memory she had actually become physically ill. Dr. Simmons found her in much worse condition than before and didn't have any doubt that her illness was very real.

Nettie had run downstairs to hear her husband, in the parlor, shouting at one of the house slaves. The slave, whose name Nettie could never recall, left the room quickly. Dudley's face was dusky red when he turned to his wife.

"Calm down, my dear, or you'll find yourself with the apoplexy," Nettie said. "I take it that you've sent for Simmons."

"The doctor? Certainly." Dudley swallowed. "I also sent for that nigger bastard, that Hannibal. It turns out that he's escaped."

"Oh?" Nettie was calm, and the beginnings of a smile quirked her lips. "Did it happen this afternoon?"

"As far as the house boys know, yes, it did. How did you guess, Nettie?"

"It occurred to me that Leola knew it would happen and she wasn't quite condemning a man to death."

"I simply don't know what you're talking about," Dudley grumbled. "You must hate our daughter very much if you don't grieve for her in this terrible situation."

" 'Hate'? No, on the contrary, it gives me some small hope for the child now that I know the slave escaped this afternoon. Our Leola isn't completely lost to human decency."

"I don't understand you, Nettie. There are times when you seem to think of yourself as the Delphic Oracle."

"I'll make myself absolutely clear if you won't jump up in anger and hit the ceiling," Nettie said, her own temper beginning to show. "I have no doubt that Leola and the black boy went through an experience, but I don't think she was as unwilling as she lets on."

"Are you mad?" Dudley stared at her. "I won't hear such talk under my roof."

"Can't you guess what makes me think so? Didn't her attitudes up there strike you, either? Or don't you want to tell yourself the truth?"

"I won't hear this talk," Dudley said, wheeling towards the door. "I'm going out."

"And when can I expect you back?"

"I don't know."

Nettie waited until he was at the door, then asked:

"Am I to cope with Dr. Simmons by myself?"

"You're fully capable of it."

"Am I not to be told where you can be reached?"

"I don't know that, myself." Dudley looked back. "If by some chance you should be telling what is the truth about Leola's recent behavior, then there is one thing that she didn't take into account."

"Are you referring to your capacity to keep a grudge, Dudley? Is that what you mean?"

"Well, I wouldn't put it quite like that, myself," Dudley pointed out. "What I mean is that I intend to find this nigger Hannibal and to kill him. With my bare hands, if necessary."

Nettie looked at her husband's grimly set jaw and hard eyes. "Yes," she murmured, "I think that you really do mean it. I'm feeling a little sorry for that colored boy, already, in spite of what he did."

CHAPTER 6

Hannibal ran as if he had never done anything else in his life. He didn't think, didn't stop to eat or take care of himself. All he did was to keep on running. If the thought had occurred to him, he would have said that he planned to run till he dropped and not a moment less.

He followed a dirt road that gleamed under the Alabama sun. He had learned how to pace himself when he ran. He must have run past a town, not wanting to hide himself there. It would have been too easy to notice him. He didn't know where to go or what to do. There was nobody to tell him. This, of course, was what freedom meant, but it was scary, too. Lord knew it was scary.

He didn't stop running until he fell. He tried to get up, but found it hard. He was next to a hay bale, though, and the shelter it offered would do for him till a little while passed and he could get up.

He drew a deep breath, which wasn't easy, and closed his eyes. The next thing he knew it was close to evening. He decided that night was the time for running and day the time for resting. He would run further.

He stood up and simply collapsed. At first he thought somebody had pushed him down, but then he realized that he simply could no longer stand. He would have to stay where he was, unless he wanted to be caught.

He got to his hands and knees, trying to crawl. He couldn't do it. His knees and hands weren't holding him.

He crawled along the ground, anxious to make more time and get as far away as possible.

"What's that?" a voice asked.

The voice belonged to somebody who was white and very young.

"It's a man." This was a white child's voice. "What are you doing here, mister man? What game is this?"

Hannibal turned his head to one side. Two children were there, a white boy and a white girl. As he stared, not able to talk, the children dropped down to their hands and knees and began to crawl with him. They wanted to be part of the game, of course, whatever it might be.

He couldn't talk. He tried hard enough, making his lips wet and actually clearing his throat. The words wouldn't come. The girl child was beginning to look at him a little strangely. The one way to keep these children quiet was to say something, but Hannibal didn't know what to say.

Sure enough, the little girl's face started to pucker as if she was going to cry.

Back of them an older woman's voice asked:

"What *is* the matter with you two children, getting your best clothes dirty like—?"

She stopped herself, seeing Hannibal. She was a fair-skinned young woman in her twenties, and she wore a dress that came down only to her knees. Bright red hair peeped out from under a cloth bonnet with a frayed string. The tip of her nose was red from the sun. She spoke different from most whites Hannibal had heard, but he could understand what she was saying.

At her look, Hannibal moved no further. He simply didn't have the strength any longer. He sank down to the earth and lay breathing quietly.

In a different tone of voice the woman said, "Children, go into the house. Immediately! And don't look back!"

Hannibal found his tongue when the children were out

55

of earshot. "I didn't hurt them, ma'am. I won't hurt anybody. All I want is to be on my way."

She asked quietly, "Can you walk?"

"Not so as to notice."

"How many hours have you been on the move?"

"I just don't know, ma'am. I can't figure out nothing 'bout time."

The woman looked from left to right, probably wanting to find help so she could put the runaway slave into chains. Hannibal tried to get up to hands and knees again at least, but couldn't manage that much even now. He had simply become exhausted and was able to do no more.

The woman said, "You'd better crawl back to the hay bale. It's sure to hide you until you get some of your strength back."

"Ma'am?" Hannibal couldn't believe his ears. "Are you saying you—you'd *help* me?"

"We'll try. Are you able to get back to the bale of hay over there?"

"Yes, ma'am. I'll get there myself. Swear I will."

He didn't want her to touch him; it might not be understood by anybody passing by. He never would know just how he found the strength to crawl back along fiery ground over to where the hay bale had been placed.

"Wait there," she said. "It won't be long."

As her steps retreated toward some house that Hannibal couldn't see, he began to get second thoughts about being helped by a white woman. She might be keeping him in one place till she was able to call for help to put him back into chains.

He decided that whatever it might cost, he wouldn't be found here when she came looking for him again. He tried to get to his hands and knees, but couldn't do it. He couldn't make himself crawl along the ground, either; there wasn't power enough in his hands to move him.

All the same he had gone a little way past the bale when he heard steps again. The woman was alone. She was carrying a bone-white cup in her hands.

"Here, you need this." He looked down at the water inside. The woman raised the cup to his lips, but Hannibal didn't want to be treated like he was sick. He reached for the cup himself and, holding it, spilled more than half of the precious water.

The woman smiled at him as she took the cup back, maybe because he had been a chuckleheaded fool.

"Do you want some more?"

He did, but he wouldn't put her to the trouble. Not for a runaway like himself.

"You wait there until it becomes dark and then we'll take you inside and find a place for you. For a while, at least, and until we can put you in touch with—well, you'll see. Try to get some rest. I don't want to be seen bringing you food in case some passerby along the road happens to notice. You'll just have to wait until it's totally dark. I'm sorry, as I say, but there isn't any help for it."

"Yes, ma'am."

"By the way, what's your name?"

He recognized a possible trap. "Joe, ma'am. My name is Joe."

"All right, Joe. Try to rest, now."

She had brought him water, that was true; but it might be that all she wanted was to keep his suspicions lulled before the sheriff's men reached him and put chains on him. There were plenty of blacks he wouldn't have trusted not to spit on his grave. Why under the sun should he trust a white woman?

But he couldn't move. He was probably going to have to lie there and wait until she put him in touch, as she said, with somebody or other. Probably with the sheriff's men. He had tried to get away. He had done what a human being could do, but there was no more energy in him.

It didn't take long before he heard a man's steps at the side of the woman's. Hannibal flapped feebly with both hands, realizing again that he couldn't move without help.

The woman said, "There he is, Perry. A runaway, of course."

"A runaway, of course," the man said.

He came into sight near the woman. He was like no sheriff that Hannibal had ever seen or could imagine. There were no cuffs in sight or chains or even a gun. He was the same age as the woman, and smoked a pipe. He kept his hands in pockets and rocked back and forth on his heels.

"His name is Joe," the woman said, repeating Hannibal's lie, "but he can't talk too much."

"Looks at least half-dead," the white man agreed, exactly as if Hannibal couldn't hear "I'll need go into town and get the sheriff, I suppose."

"Perry, we have to help him. It's a matter of conscience."

"Conscience? A girl like you comes down from the North and marries out here and gets the damnedest ideas in tarnation. It's foolish to hide a slave, and dangerous besides."

"We can't let him go on like this."

"Martha, if the sheriff's people find out what you want to do, then the two of us might go to jail. Even if we don't, we can never hold up our heads again in decent society."

"There can't be much decent society here if it would agree to turning in a slave," Martha said spiritedly. "And I'm not sure I wouldn't include my own husband."

"Oh now, let's not get into a ruckus," her husband protested. "Certainly not on account of one nigg—"

58

"Don't say that word." Martha shuddered. "I *hate* that word."

"There's not a thing wrong with it. Everybody around here calls 'em niggers, just like they call you a woman and me a man. That's what they are, Martha! Blame it, don't be so all-fired touchy about nothing at all."

"How can you call it nothi—?"

"All right, dear, just a moment. I take it you want us to help this not-too-savory specimen. All right. For your sake, I'll do it. After dark, I'll bring him something to eat."

"We'll take him into the house and give him a bed."

"A field nigger in the house? Why he could run off with every piece of property we've got. Niggers are all like magpies, dear. If you had been brought up with them, you'd know it as well as I do."

"In the house," Martha insisted.

"You'd risk the children's lives, too?"

"There's no risk."

The man grew rigid. "Maybe we'll talk about it later."

"We'll talk about it now if we have to. And you know what else has to be done? We have to put him in touch with—"

"Hang it, Martha, you're going too far."

He nearly ran away to hide himself in his defeat at the woman's hands. Martha stayed behind long enough to take further notice of Hannibal's general condition.

"It'll be all right now," she said comfortingly. "You'll see."

She left Hannibal to worry and try to work up his strength. He wished he could. When darkness fell, the woman and man came out to him again.

Perry shifted the pipe in his mouth. "Come with me," he said.

Hannibal couldn't get up. Perry watched impatiently. Martha said, "I'll help you."

59

Perry snapped at her, "Don't you touch him—hear me?"

"I'll do whatever has to be done."

She moved closer to Hannibal, but Perry suddenly pushed her out of the way. Rather than wilt under his wife's glare, he turned to Hannibal and hunched down on his knees.

"Put a hand around my shoulder. I'll help you inside."

With Perry's help, Hannibal limped around the hay bale and over to a small house that looked neat in its blue and white paint. The front door was open.

Perry suddenly said to him, "Turn left, you! The direction away from me."

Martha looked shocked. "You're taking him to the cellar! How could you?"

"Get some food for him," Perry snapped. "Don't make so many complaints."

He was taken to a room that was big and damp. There was a small chair and what looked like a bed in the far corner. Hannibal hadn't ever slept on a bed, and he couldn't imagine it was supposed to be for him to use.

The chair was at one side of a rickety table. Perry let go of him as soon as he got to the chair, so Hannibal was sure he was supposed to sit down on that. He'd have given almost anything to try the old cot that looked to him like a good warm luxurious bed.

Carefully he sat down on the hard chair. Martha brought him parts of a chicken, which he ate with his hands. There were some hard things on the dish, one that looked like little knives and one that looked like a small shovel. They were too hard to eat, so he left them alone.

Perry snickered when he tried to eat the cutlery.

Martha said, "If you hadn't been taught different, you'd eat with your hands, too, and you'd know nothing about cutlery."

Hannibal felt the warmth in his middle when he was

60

finished eating and he wanted nothing more than to get some sleep.

"I'm glad you didn't bring him a knife, like I told you not to," Perry said, his voice growing more dim in Hannibal's ears as Hannibal closed his eyes and nodded.

Martha suddenly asked, "What are you doing?"

"Making sure he doesn't do a magpie on us," Perry said. "When you're dealing with persons of color, you can't be too careful."

"He's too tired to steal," Martha pointed out. "Can't you see he'll be asleep in no time?"

"So it won't make any difference to him if he can't get out because the door is bolted on the other side."

"Very well, I know better than to try and convince you about something," Martha said, having decided to give in on one minor issue now that she had won all the important points. She turned to Hannibal. "Good night, Joe."

Hannibal remembered the name he had given as his own. "Good night, ma'am."

Perry said nothing. He made a point of bolting the door from the outside when nobody else was in the big room. Through a daze Hannibal heard the man's voice raised, maybe at his wife's insistence.

"Good night," Perry called out to him. "Good night, you."

Hannibal staggered over to the rickety cot and touched it in the middle. It looked too nice to sleep on, too soft, too rich.

On his first night as a free man, Hannibal slept on the floor beside the rickety old cot.

CHAPTER 7

The noise of the door being unbolted woke him. By the time the door had been opened, he was wide awake and he remembered where he was. He wondered, too, who it was that Martha had said she was going to put him in contact with, and felt a moment's fear that the sheriff was on the other side of the door. Sunlight poured down on him as the door opened, and not till he made out the sight of Martha's dress did he tell himself that the man next to her was Perry and not some local sheriff.

"There's no need to worry any more," Martha said, smiling as she advanced. "In a little while, your big problem will be as good as over."

Hannibal looked wary. Had she sent for the sheriff after all?

Perry, after noticing with contempt that Hannibal had ignored the cot and slept on the floor, said to his wife, "I swear I wouldn't do this if not for you."

"Any reason is good enough," Martha said promptly, easing the flat board with dishes down to the table. "Fill yourself with something to eat, Joe. This will be an important day for you."

Hannibal responded to the name he had given her and ate a breakfast of grits and some milk. He had been hungry, but he lost his appetite as he wondered what they were going to do to him next.

The man didn't say a word. When the breakfast was finished, Hannibal looked up slowly.

"Guess I'll be on my way," he said. "Thanks very much for everything."

"Not *that* fast," Perry said, and Hannibal told himself that the time had come for him to fight against being turned in to the sheriff's men and brought back to Safe Harbor in chains. "You'll be going out of here to freedom, but only after a little while."

"To—" He didn't believe it for a moment. He blinked and gasped. Something seemed to hurt him, suddenly, and he didn't know what it was.

Perry said, "I'll take you to somebody who can get you up North, where you can't be brought back as a slave. I suppose you've heard about the underground railroad."

Hannibal didn't know what either of the last words might mean. He shook his head furiously, then decided he was acting like a fool and shook his head more calmly.

Martha said to Perry, "You'd better take him along, now."

"Yes, if we're going."

She smiled at him. "Goodbye, Joe."

As Perry moved to the door and said impatiently, "Come on now," Hannibal waited. His eyes rested on Martha.

"Thank you, ma'am," he said quietly. "I'm sorry there isn't anything I can do to pay you back, but thanks very much."

"That's all right, Joe."

He said, "Hannibal, ma'am. That's my real name. I didn't want to say it before, but that's the only thing I can do to thank you for what you did for me. My name is Hannibal."

She understood how much it had cost a suspicious black man to tell any part of the truth about himself. She looked away from him and toward her husband.

63

"Please take Hannibal with you, dear," she said. "The sooner he's free, the better."

Perry nodded, then led Hannibal to a hay wagon. Dazed at the nearness of freedom, Hannibal was going to climb onto the buckboard. Perry stopped him swiftly.

"Are you crazy, boy? Get into the hay and keep quiet."

It had to be done that way, of course. Hannibal found that the hay made him itchy, but there was no help for it as the wagon scraped along country roads.

He never knew how far they traveled before the wagon stopped and Perry got off the buckboard and walked around to the back.

"Out you get," he called.

Hannibal climbed out of the wagon at last, leaving hay shoots on the earth around him and sweeping himself free with the flat of a hard hand. He was in front of a farmhouse, the only one in sight, that he had never seen before.

"Go in there," Perry said, pointing to the black door. "You'll have no trouble with Sam Rinders. He runs slaves up to the North all the time, and he's the best friend your people ever had in this neck of the woods."

"Thanks, Mister Perry," Hannibal said, knowing that to help him had cost the white man some pride.

Perry said, almost angrily, "You owe it all to my wife, dammit!"

"I know she pushed you into it," Hannibal agreed. "What I'm thanking you for is that you let yourself get pushed."

Perry shut his eyes tightly and shook his head as if he wished that the last moments hadn't taken place. Then he opened them and said shrewdly:

"You afraid to go in there, boy?"

"N-no."

"I'll take you."

"I can go by myself," Hannibal said with dignity, but he couldn't make himself move.

"Perry knocked on the door, opened it, and called out, "You've got another guest, Sam."

"Bring him in," a cheerful voice said. "Let's see the cut of his jib."

Perry stood aside as the black man walked into the house. The floor was cruel to his bare feet, and his eyes squinted at the dimness. A man sitting in the far corner, book in hand, got up and came over to him. Hannibal pulled back, but he saw that the man's hand was drawn out towards him.

"I'm Sam Rinders, friend," he said. "Put it there."

Hannibal had never shaken hands with a white man before. Sam Rinders' hand was heavy and his grip was firm. He was a heavy man, not as big as Hannibal. His teeth were bad. There wasn't a hair on his head. His complexion took the sun badly, it seemed, and was probably always red.

Hannibal didn't like a white man who was too friendly. The best friend to Negroes in this area simply put his back up, and Hannibal wished he knew why.

"What is your name?" Sam Rinders boomed. "Mine is Sam, but I guess you know that."

"I'm Joe," Hannibal said, and looked to Perry in hopes that the other white man would keep the truth to himself.

Perry shrugged, but didn't make any comment.

"Well, Joe, you'll stay here till it's dark and then you'll set out on your travels to little old New York, if that's where you want to go. I hear a lot of good things about Pennsylvania, too, but I guess that New York is best for you after all."

"I don't know what I'll be doing, sir," Hannibal said.

"Have you eaten?"

"Yes, sir."

65

Sam Rinders chuckled. "You don't have to call me 'sir', young fellow. I'm Sam."

Hannibal nodded, but it struck him that "young fellow" sounded very much like "boy." At least it meant the same thing.

"I'll show you to your room, Joe. You can take a load off your mind and get some sleep."

Perry had stayed behind for a longer time than Hannibal could have expected him to. Now he cleared his throat.

"Everything's all right now—uh, Joe?"

"Yes, Mister Perry. And thanks again for all the things you did."

"That's all right." Perry hesitated. "Good luck, Joe."

And he left without looking back of him. Hannibal wished he could have liked Sam Rinders as much as he liked Mister Perry. It was hard for him to trust anybody who behaved as if things were just fine and that the two of them were friends. An old slave at Master Dudley's had always said that the fellow to look out after was your friend for the reason that you were already on guard against your enemy.

Sam Rinders wasn't quite as friendly toward him when Mister Perry left, but he led Hannibal into a small room with a cot. Hannibal found himself looking at Sam Rinders' shoes, which pounded against the floor.

"Now, Joe, is there anything else you want? Anything at all? Just name it."

Hannibal asked, "Anything at all? Well, I sure would like to have me two of those."

Sam laughed. "None of the shoes I've got would fit you, young fellow. Sorry."

Hannibal was going to repeat the words "anything at all", but decided against that. On the way out, Sam Rinders suddenly turned and looked Hannibal up and down.

"Strong as a bull, aren't you?"

"I'm strong," Hannibal said, nodding warily.

66

"Oh, don't look as if I was going to ask you to do some chore," Sam Rinders said easily.

"If you want a chore done, I'll do it," Hannibal said quickly. At least he would know that Sam Rinders wasn't one of those man-lovers. Sam's looking him up and down that way had put the notion into Hannibal's mind.

"No chore, young fellow. I just happened to be—um, thinking out loud."

Sam left the door open, but Hannibal closed it and put a chair against it. He sat down on this cot, which he guessed was soft. He stared at the door, as if worried by what would happen when Sam Rinders tried to open it. After all, Sam Rinders could suggest that if Hannibal did what he wanted then Hannibal would get to the North. Hannibal started to sweat just thinking about the choice.

But Sam Rinders made no move to come into the room. At one time he heard the big man getting closer to the door and he braced himself for trouble, but Sam Rinders only knocked.

"You want some grub? Come and get it."

Hannibal would have given considerable not to leave that room, but he was getting suspicious of everything that happened now that had never happened to him before. It had to stop now, and he meant to stop it.

He opened the door carefully, looking to left and right. There was only one table, and two settings.

"We'll eat together," Sam Rinders said cheerfully. "Plain food, but good. Doesn't rot the stomach."

Hannibal decided against eating. He never knew if Sam Rinders might put something in there that would make him weak enough not to put up a fight in case Sam Rinders wanted the other thing. He drank the water, and took a gob of food in his mouth when Rinders was looking, made believe he was chewing on it and spat it into his hand and then into his pocket later on as soon as Rinders was looking down to his plate.

67

"I suppose you're a little bothered by eating at the same table with a white man," Sam Rinders said easily. "You must think I'm crazy to get into this sort of trouble in general when I don't really need trouble."

Hannibal said, "I don't know, Mis—Sam, I mean."

"I've been helping Negroes get up North for a long time now, and nobody ever says a word against me. You would think that the sheriff knows and the others do. In that case, why don't I get some hard knocks from them? Wouldn't you like to know why?"

"Yes, if you want to tell me."

"It's because I'm doing a service for the slave owners," Sam Rinders said. "Look here. Your weak slave, your older slave, isn't generally watched like the young and strong ones. A lot of them can get away and they do. Well, to get rid of a weak slave who isn't doing much work because he can't, well, that isn't a bad thing for the slave owner. Do you understand me, Joe?"

"Yes."

Sam Rinders leaned forward to talk. Hannibal made a point of obviously drawing back. Sam Rinders didn't seem to notice, though.

"The master appreciates not having to pay for a weak slave any longer, of course," Sam Rinders said, "and the slave can end his life in freedom, which he wants. Of course he becomes a public charge more often than not, but that's the North's worry. The point is that I'm keeping both sides happy."

Hannibal asked carefully, "What happens when a strong and powerful slave comes to you for help?"

"Then and only then, as it happens, am I taking a risk," Sam Rinders said. "But there are ways of cutting down on risks, Joe, or at least making them easier to take. Believe me, I know all the answers in this business. You're in good hands."

When the meal was finished, Sam Rinders said, "It's

not so light now and we'll be leaving in a little while. You want to take a walk on my grounds?"

"No, I think I'll get some sleep."

"Well, that's good." Sam Rinders chuckled. "I was afraid you didn't trust me, but if you can sleep at my place it's a sure sign that you've changed your mind."

Hannibal smiled at Sam Rinders and went into the small room he had been given. He dumped the food in his pockets out the window, which he closed and put a chair against. He put another chair against the door. There was a trio of tacks on the wall, and he put them point end up on the chair against the window. Then he dropped into the cot.

He slept more deeply than he would have expected. He was with Miriam again, touching her, holding hands, making love. They were interrupted by Rufus, the fat slave at Master Dudley's, and then by Sarah Jane. For some reason Sarah Jane was turning white as Hannibal looked at her.

He heard some sounds. At one point he heard a chair falling over. He started to move in the bed when there were some footsteps, and he was hit on the head and didn't know what was happening. He remembered putting his hands in front of his sex, but then everything turned into nothing.

Vaguely he heard a horse clip-clopping along a road. He thought he could smell the horse. He felt himself in the middle of the air, only he was hooked to something at his legs and one shoulder.

He didn't come to until his body landed against a wooden floor. He called out and opened his eyes weakly. His head was bursting and it was hard to see things.

He was in a badly lighted room. Sam Rinders stood with fists on hips. He was looking at another white man who stared down at Hannibal. The other white man looked heavy, and his nose was red from too much whiskey. He carried a gun, which was pointed lazily at Hannibal.

"No need to do that to any of my young fellows," Sam Rinders was saying. "They all behave as soon as they wake up. They're pretty much shocked by what's been happening."

"I guess he'll do," the white man said. "He looks strong enough."

Hannibal's first conscious thought was that he was to work and not do any man-loving. He nearly felt relieved.

Sam Rinders looked over at Hannibal. "I really hate to do this sort of thing, young fellow, but I only do it when there's somebody young and strong coming to my place. Very few people who don't own slaves know about how I handle that sort of thing. I've really helped a lot of your people, young fellow, and you ought to be grateful to me."

Hannibal spat, but didn't suppose Sam Rinders saw it or cared. If not for the gun pointed at him, he would have stood up and choked the life out of the sorrowful looking Rinders.

"Now," he said, turning to the other man, "you make the identification."

"Certainly. This slave is named Ezekiel, and he's a runaway of mine. My son will testify to that and so will my overseer. You'll get the hundred-dollar reward I put out for him in the first place."

"I appreciate that," Sam Rinders said carefully. "It's right good of you. But I think you ought to make it two hundred on account of certain irregularities."

"Blackmail, but in the circumstances I'll pay it."

"I ought to tell you that this one says his name is Joe. Not that it changes anything."

"He would tell you his name is Daniel Webster if he knew who old Dan'l is," the slave owner said. "I'll make it two hundred, Sam. He looks like he might work out."

"Oh, he'll be fine," Sam Rinders said cheerfully.

"Knows his place, this one does. Hell, he's sure been a slave his whole life."

"You!" the slave owner turned to Hannibal. "I'm having you taken out to my slave pens. If you give any trouble around here, boy, you'll get your ass whipped good. Now, move like you're told!"

CHAPTER 8

Dudley Stark sat in a corner with some slave owners to whom he had just been introduced. The ball was going on around them, and the talk of these men concerned him, but his mind was somewhere else.

He had come out to this party because Nettie had insisted. His wife had said that Leola needed some entertainment after her recent illness, and a ball would be just what Dr. Simmons would have ordered if he had thought of it.

Leola, however, was staying close to her father and listening to the conversation all around him. She had swept the ballroom with an experienced eye and decided that the boys didn't amount to much.

Nettie, who had insisted on their coming here, was enjoying herself. She was talking to friends she hadn't seen in years. She had adapted one of the new Parisian styles by pulling her hair back. It didn't look as well on her as it might have looked on Leola, but it was brand-new in Alabama—or at least that was what Nettie had hoped.

With the exception of Dudley, people in the ballroom seemed happy. Dudley sat, drink in one hand and cigar in the other, listening to the talk that swirled around him.

"Nothing to worry about from Washington any more," one of the men was saying. "Not for the moment, at any rate. There'll be no slavery debate during this session."

"There shouldn't be one at all," another one said.

"Those baboons in Congress are always prying into what's none of their blamed business."

"Of course. A man's enterprises ought to be left free from prying eyes." He turned to Dudley. "Don't you agree?"

"Yes, yes," Dudley said distractedly.

"Does the sight of all these pretty girls make your mind wander?"

"Not at all, or at least not more than you might expect. I was thinking about something else."

He was remembering the tall dark slave who had brutalized his daughter and whom he hadn't found yet. The slave had simply disappeared into thin air.

Dudley had hunted with patience and persistence, asking people who were supposed to be part of the underground railroad as well as other slave owners. He had gone out of the immediate location, in fact, and talked to people in far-off parts of the state. There had been one fellow, a man named Samuel Rinders, who had looked interested for a while, but he said he couldn't give any help because he didn't know anything about the slave Dudley described. Dudley had questioned Samuel Rinders pretty severely and had even threatened him with horsewhipping, but the man hadn't budged from his claims that he didn't know anything at all about a big strong slave called Hannibal.

The harder it became for Dudley, the more firmly he made up his mind to get hold of that slave and kill him, painfully if possible.

The dark man at his side, a heavy man with a nose made red by drinking, suddenly said, "I don't think I've ever met you before, Stark. Those of us who are in the same field of enterprise ought to know each other better."

Dudley nodded, but he didn't agree. He hated the notion of having anything at all in common with most of the slave owners he had met.

73

"It becomes harder as time goes on for any plantation owner to make a proper living," the man said. "Slaves aren't easy to find, heaven knows, and as soon as you buy one he develops the most amazing range of illnesses. Sometimes, by heavens, I think that they cover the whole range of the medical encyclopedia."

"It does happen," Dudley admitted.

"If they're healthy, they won't work," the man said. "If you find a strong, brawny slave who'll work it's like finding a mine of gold."

"Agreed." Dudley couldn't put the picture of hard-muscled black Hannibal out of his mind, and especially not the idea of Hannibal touching Leola in this place or in that place and being on top of her as he forced his will on the hapless white girl who was Dudley Stark's daughter.

"Every so often, though," the red-nosed slave owner said, "fortune favors you. Let me give you an example drawn from my own personal experience. There's a scalawag who smuggles slaves up North. Generally he smuggles the weak and scrawny slaves who can't do too much work, and they're no loss to the community. But every so often a good strong slave come to him."

"Does he turn the slave back?"

"Yes, if he knows where the slave came from," the red-nosed plantation owner said. "Otherwise he goes to one of us and for a few dollars he sells the slave to that one. Let's say that a slave of yours recently died and you've still got the papers. You go to Sam, and then as soon as a chance comes, he'll—"

Dudley jumped. "Would this be a rascal named Samuel Rinders?"

"Yes, it would. Do you know him?"

Dudley was thinking that with this information he could find out what Rinders knew about Hannibal. It would be his first chore in the morning. He would shake Rinders till the man's store-bought teeth rattled.

74

He was too excited to hear what else the slave owner was saying. He turned to Leola as if to tell her that she'd soon get her revenge, but Leola suddenly turned away. There was excitement in the girl's face as she listened to the red-nosed man, but she tamped it down and began looking around. A house slave was taking trays from the sideboard.

Leola approached him: "Who is that thick-bellied gentleman sitting over there? The man with the red nose."

The slave looked, then smiled back. He was a middle-aged darkie with gray hair and strong hands. "Master David, Miss. He's a good master."

"I suppose that one of his children, at least, is at the ball or he wouldn't be here himself."

"Mister Colin, Miss." The slave hesitated. "Master David is a good master."

"What's his last name?"

"Ramsey, Miss. A good mas—"

She supposed that the slave was worried about being sent back to the fields. Maybe he had been threatened with such punishment.

"I'll tell his son that you said so," she smiled. "What's the son's name? His first name?"

"Mister Colin, Miss. Mister Colin Ramsey." And again, "Master David is a good man—"

Leola turned away, then glanced back and thanked the slave politely. Colin Ramsey, who was pointed out to her by one of the merry-makers, was a red-haired lad who looked younger than Leola. At the moment his attention was taken by a chit of a girl who had dressed herself with no color or flash. The girl's eyes were strong and lustrous, though, and she looked worshipfully at Colin Ramsey. Leola didn't approve of that. No girl should wear her heart on her sleeve.

The girl showed no signs of letting young Colin Ramsey go, so that Leola advanced on them. She approached in such a way that Colin Ramsey was bound

75

to see her out of the corner of an eye. When she stopped in front of him, their eyes met.

"Didn't you promise me this dance?" she asked gaily.

"Did I?" He looked vague. "Maybe it's somebody who looks like me and promised you the dance."

"I'm sure it was you."

"Why, if you say so, it's an honor."

They danced together, Leola moving her body so that it was closer to Colin Ramsey than strictly necessary. Colin was flattered by the attention of an older and pretty woman, and he could see half a dozen envious glances thrown at him from the other male dancers on the floor.

"Does your daddy have many slaves?" she asked, as if to make conversation.

"I've never counted."

"What's the plantation called? Have I seen it?"

"Called? Its name is Bon Repos. That's French for good rest, though I've never had muct rest there. My great-great grandfather named it that. He's supposed to have been a blackbirder and he probably needed the rest after smuggling niggers into the country."

"My father owns Safe Harbor," she said. "I wonder if your father's place is bigger than mine."

"His place covers—"

"I can't remember numbers of acres."

"Well, maybe I can show it to you sometime. I'd be delighted to show you Bon Repos one of these days."

"Now?"

"Well, it's too late."

"It's never too late for something if you really want to do it, Colin. Surely you know that."

"You couldn't see anything now, it's so dark. The slaves would be fast asleep, for one thing, and—"

"Tomorrow morning, then? Bright and early?"

Young Colin Ramsey didn't have any idea how he had been trapped into this. One of his pimples itched fiercely, but he couldn't scratch it at the moment.

"It's—uh, nice that you're so interested."

"Lee. That's what my friends call me."

"Well then, Lee, it's nice to know you're interested and I'd be glad to take you on a tour of Bon Repos. Maybe sometime next week, when things are a little less hectic than they are right now."

"I'd like to see Bon Repos tomorrow morning, Colin. One of the slaves out here—that one walking past with the tray—told me that your daddy is a good master, and I like to see happy slaves. Besides, Colin, a girl's whims shouldn't be denied."

"Very well," Colin said stiffly, knowing he was trapped and more than half-hoping for some adventure he could talk about in secret to his friends. "My carriage will call for you at one-thirty in the afternoon."

"Better make it seven-thirty in the morning," Leola said. "That way, I'll be able to confine my sightseeing to the morning."

She said it in such a way as to indicate that the most wonderful things would happen in the afternoon.

"Y-yes, of course," Colin Ramsey said. "Bright and early tomorrow morning, my carriage will call for you."

Leola appeared in riding clothes, saying that she assumed she would see Bon Repos on horseback. Colin, who imagined a more intimate sort of tour and was nursing a headache because he'd had a few drinks too many, gave in to her. He wouldn't take out a horse, though, with the result that he rode in a carriage and Leola on horseback.

The use of a carriage wasn't as helpful as Colin had hoped. When Leola wanted to know something about the grounds, she would turn to him and ask; and he had to shout to make himself heard. It was bad for his headache and not very much better for his voice.

Sometimes he shouted about points of interest as they passed, but Leola didn't pay much attention. She was

77

riding a black filly with white spots and seemed more interested in the slave quarters than any other part of the establishment. She kept asking questions about the dingy pair of buildings which housed the slave pens and couldn't keep her eyes from them.

"Won't you take me over to see them close up?"

He did it unwillingly, and saw that she was irritated because no slaves were at the pens but only in the fields.

"I want to see the fields now," Leola said.

Colin made the journey a longer one in order to show her that much more of Bon Repos, but she seemed impatient and changed the subject.

"Do you buy many things for the plantation? Negroes, for instance?"

Colin's father did all the slave-buying, but Colin said off-handedly, "Once in a while. Of course you have to be careful, even at Bon Repos. We have a lot of good niggers here, believe me. Been with us for a long time. But every so often they go wild."

"Really?" Leola's eyes were round as saucers. "I wouldn't think they'd do too much damage. They aren't that strong after a day in the fields."

"Most of them aren't, but last night—well, never mind. That's not the sort of thing a young lady should hear."

Leola, of course, insisted.

"There's really not that much to tell," Colin shouted from the buckboard, although Leola came closer to him for once in order to make it easier for him to talk. "Somebody gets 'em all upset and they go on a rampage and break things and what not. One time they hurt an overseer so bad that we needed to let him go. Last night, well, everybody was a little relaxed, and my daddy went over to the slave pens to find 'em staggering 'round and calling names and so on."

" 'Staggering around'?"

"I don't know how they do it, but they manage to make some kind of a malt drink that's very strong," Colin said.

"They were all shaking their fists at my daddy, but they couldn't walk straight. One of them actually began to relieve himself as soon as my daddy came in sight. In fact, I think he—well—intended it to touch him. Daddy, who won't go near the slave pens without he carries a pistol, hauled it out and now we've got us one slave less."

"How did the others take on after that?"

"With one exception, they was too drunk to do anything about it," Colin said. "They just shook their fists and shouted and cursed and spat. You know, like monkeys. Niggers and monkeys is pretty much the same."

"What about the one exception?" Leola asked, her eyes shining.

"Well, he's pretty new here. He's a big black buck, that one. He came charging at my daddy, right in the teeth of the pistol. He knocked that pistol out of daddy's hand. He raised a hand to daddy as if he was going to hit him, but changed his mind at the last moment. He knew he would be hanged for that, I'm sure, so he didn't do it. He just kicked the pistol away."

"Didn't your daddy try and hit him?"

"My daddy wouldn't soil his hands on a nigger," Colin said righteously.

Leola nodded, although she couldn't imagine the stubby David Ramsey being able to do much damage to an aroused Hannibal.

"My daddy just walked off," Colin said. "The other monkeys were shouting and screaming and shaking their fists and what all else. My daddy walked away from them."

"I suppose the slave who knocked the pistol out of your daddy's hand has been dealt with," Leola said. She gestured. "What's that over there? The whipping post? Or is there more than one whipping post at Bon Repos?"

Colin strained his head to look where she pointed, rather than at the road itself. It was a mistake. The horse nearly lost his balance, bringing the wagon partly down.

Colin, thoroughly shaken, eased the horse to a stop, calmed it and got out and looked at the damage.

"Leg is all right," he said, turning from the animal with a sigh of relief. But the wagon trembled under his touch and he got out to look it over. "This will need a little fixing. If you wait on for a few minutes, I'll jigger things around so they'll be all right."

Leola gave a bewitching smile. "I can ride around and pick you up again. Meanwhile I can see more of this beautiful plantation of yours, and it really is beautiful."

"But Leola—Miss Leola—Lee!"

Leola had spurred her pony, and was glad to be on the way by herself.

The ground sloped gently, and her pony moved like a veteran. The rise that followed drained the pony's breath for a time, though. As for Leola, for some reason she wasn't sure about, she had begun to breathe with difficulty.

Over the rise she heard a sound that was like a thunder-clap, followed by another sound just like it. She turned half around till she could look to her right, where the sound was coming from. That was when she started to shiver.

The whipping post was thin, so that a man could put his arms around it but not expect it to carry any of his weight. The post was no bigger than Hannibal, who was tied to it. She could see the bare back of a man with a whip. The man was a Negro, much to Leola's surprise, and he was sweating. She had tried not to see the gashes on Hannibal's back.

A white man demanded, "Put your strength into it."

"Yes, sir."

"Otherwise I'll put you up there and do the job my-self."

The white man stood at the right of the Negro with the whip. He was dressed in rumpled white. From the aura of uncertain authority that came from him, Leola took it for granted that he was the overseer.

"But he's bleeding," the Negro with the whip protested. "He's bleeding real bad."

"If he wasn't strong enough to do the work of three men, he'd stop bleeding after he was tied," the overseer said. "Give it to him once more."

The Negro, tired, raised the whip hand. The tip of the lash came down solidly across Hannibal's broad back. The noise it made was like that of a bullet leaving a pistol.

"Enough for now," the overseer said. "No, don't untie the knots. He'll do where he is for a while."

In the warm weather, the words carried to Leola, who waited quietly. A shaggy dog approached blood drops on the earth and began to lick them away. The Negro who had used that whip turned to the dog and eased it away from the blood drops. He did it with soft words and the lightest pressure of a hand. At no time did he use force against the animal.

"Back to work for you," the overseer told the Negro.

The Negro walked off, the overseer behind him. Leola watched the overseer's back become smaller. Then she got off her horse and approached the whipping post. The salty smell of blood invaded her nostrils.

"Hannibal," she called quietly. "Hannibal, can you hear me?"

His head stirred, but he was too weak to talk.

"I'll get you off there," she said eagerly. "You leave it to me."

She undid the ropes carefully, grateful that her nails weren't long. She had to help Hannibal step away from the post and sit down on the earth. He wouldn't lie down. His face was wet with sweat.

Leola washed the blood with water from the nearby stream, doing all she could in order to staunch the flow. Hannibal hadn't said a word.

81

At one point she stopped and nearly called out. She had been trying to stem the blood flow from a shoulder wound. She looked over a shoulder and across the scrub grass. A Negro was watching them wide-eyed.

"Oh God, I've been seen."

Hannibal spoke for the first time. "Don't worry about him. He won't do anything."

"He might tell."

"Won't."

His tone was convincing, and she realized that Hannibal couldn't talk much because of the pain. She kept sponging the wounds, pleased at the touch of his skin against hers. At one point she leaned down and kissed a wound where it wouldn't stop bleeding. There was a bright red froth on her lips, but she didn't wipe it off.

"When I was young my mother used to kiss the place where it hurt and make it well that way." She stopped herself abruptly. "Hannibal, you've got to escape."

"Yes."

"For one thing, my father is going to find out where you are and then he'll come after you and kill you."

"Just for being a runaway?"

"More than that. He thinks that you—well, I had to say something and I told him that you took bad advantage of me."

Hannibal's head was nearly turned around, but he couldn't look at her that way. She saw that he was physically affected by her touch, and the knowledge surprised and pleased her. He turned his head back and she could no longer see the physical effect. The sight of it had caused her to feel as if her throat was dry and her hands were shaking.

"So that's what you said." Hannibal sighed. "If he catches me, I'll dance on the air."

"Yes, you'll certainly hang," she agreed. "That's why you have to go."

"How?"

She gestured in the direction from which she had come and he looked where the finger pointed.

"The big house is there," he said. "I'm sure to be seen, you know."

"I was pointing to the pony," she said. The pony was the same color as the scrub grass, and it was no wonder he hadn't seen it. "Her name is Darling. You get on and ride her until you're far away, then send her back."

Her swab at a lash injury missed him because he had suddenly turned and fiercely gripped her hands in one of his. "You tell Master Dudley Stark all them lies and now you want to save my life so you shouldn't feel bad about what you did. Isn't that right?"

"If you want to call it that." She looked uneasily over his shoulder once more. "I only wish he wasn't here."

Hannibal looked around at the smooth bland-faced Negro with the gray hair. He was no more than twenty feet from them, and his eyes were nowhere else but on the two of them. Not that Leola blamed him for that.

"He'll never tell anybody," Hannibal said, turning back impatiently. "I could deck you out right here and he still wouldn't tell anybody. You don't have to worry about him."

"But I—I—" Her face was hot.

Hannibal, straightening up now, his strength partly revived through care and her closeness, said, "Maybe I should deck you out right here. If I've got the name, I ought to get the game, too."

"Not here," she said swiftly, rather than making the claim of not wanting him that way. "Not when there's somebody to see—"

It was one argument he couldn't answer, but she never got to finish making it. He had kissed her. She kissed back passionately, her tongue finding his in a loving joust. His hands were on her clothes, taking, opening, undoing.

She withdrew her lips long enough to say at last, "We'll be seen."

83

"I don't care," he whispered fiercely, "and I could get hanged for this."

It was true. He could be killed and there was a witness. The combination of risks made her pulses pound so quickly that she could hardly breathe or hear any longer. There was a pounding noise that ran clear down to the soles of her feet.

"Then hurry," a voice said. (Was it hers?) "Hurry and then run away. Even if there isn't any time we have to do it at least once."

She was on the earth and she wore nothing and her legs had been pushed apart. His hands touched her breasts knowingly, and her nipples hardened to his touch. His hands were everywhere. She was gasping. It was hard for her to see anything until the moment when that black presence hovered over her.

He was nearly stopped by the look of welcome mixed with fear that he saw on her face. This was the moment to which she had been building herself, and in a while there would be no turning back and the action was never going to be recalled.

As he hesitated, she reached up her hands and pulled him down on top of her. She felt a finger probing for the entrance to her, a finger lancing through a thicket of short and curly hair. She brought one hand back to touch his sex and insert it into her. She gasped, then, and put both hands on his brawny black arms and squeezed as if for dear life.

There was a moment of agony, followed by a long drawn out moment of bliss. She sighed softly, eyes closed.

She wanted nothing more than to relax and sleep, but it was out of the question at this time. Hannibal had eased himself out of her. He smiled, then kissed her on the forehead. She wanted to hold him and not let go, but his life was at stake.

He asked, "Are you going to say I took advantage of you this time, too?"

84

"Not this time," she said slowly, the words coming as if from far away. "I'll say I had an accident with the horse and was knocked out. When I revived, I'll say, the horse was gone. But I won't say anything if—well, if you take me with you."

"It's too dangerous, with your daddy wanting to go through plenty of trouble just to get me and hang me."

So she had ruined her own chances with Hannibal, it seemed. She wanting nothing more than to stay on this patch of earth forever, but forced herself to stand up.

"Where will you be? Where will I find you again?"

"The best thing for us both is not to see each other, ever. You know that as well as I do."

He turned his back on her and began walking in the direction of the horse. She turned toward him and spoke quietly in a voice he couldn't make out.

"I don't love you, but I do love the things we do," she murmured. "I couldn't be in love with a nigger."

CHAPTER 9

Dudley Stark had returned to the Ramsey plantation, Bon Repos. It was late morning of what was going to be a sticky day, and his temper was on a short rein. He found David Ramsey on the veranda and began to talk without introduction.

"You've got a slave of mine," he said. "You got him only the other day. His name is Hannibal. He's a runaway and I plan to hang him."

"How do you know I've got this runaway of yours?" Ramsey said after a moment. He had been scowling through a newspaper, and now he took off his reading glasses and set them down on a wide scarred table. "There's no boy named Hannibal here."

"I've been talking to Sam Rinders."

"You must have got Sam to say whatever you wanted to hear." Ramsey looked down at Dudley Stark's hands. "Do you often skin your knuckles in talk?"

"When I talk to a rascal like Sam Rinders, my knuckles start to itch."

"And of course you made them bleed by scratching them so fiercely." Ramsey was wiping his red nose with a thumb and forefinger when he stood up.

"The only slave I've got who might qualify is named Ezekiel, but he keeps saying his name is Joe. He's a strong boy, coal black, and about six feet tall."

"That's Hannibal."

"Hm. I suppose you wonder why I'm being so cooperative with you, Stark, and not denying everything. After all, even southern hospitality has got its clear-cut limits."

"He's given you some trouble, I suppose."

"I'll be glad to get rid of him," Ramsey said firmly. "A troublemaker, that one. Hanging is just about what he deserves. I'll bring a rope with me and we can do it this morning. Be an object lesson to my other niggers."

"I want him back in chains."

"We hang him at Bon Repos and you bring the body back to Safe Harbor, or have some of my boys do it," Ramsey said eagerly. "We put the body in chains. You can show it off to your boys and I can show it off to mine. It'll be an object lesson, like I say, to the whole pack of monkeys."

"Let's get to him first. We can decide it on the way there."

"Let me get my pistol and I'll be with you," his host said. "I never go near the monkeys without a pistol."

Dudley Stark waited on the sun-pocked veranda. Mental images of Hannibal hanging from a tree in the sun played around his recollection. Hannibal's face was blue in those mental pictures, his tongue white, his neck pale, his hands still raised to claw at the rope that had taken life from him.

Ramsey appeared in a few moments. He wore a horse pistol in a holster along with a flat-brimmed white hat to go with his white shirt and pants and shoes. He carried a rope in one hand.

"We'll put off the hanging," Dudley Stark said. "I want my daughter to see it, too." Ramsey looked disappointed.

They took a wagon for the fields after Ramsey declined to use the one in which Dudley Stark had come and then found out that his son was escorting some young girl about Bon Repos and using the best wagon for the purpose. He was muttering under his breath when he led Dudley to a battered wagon and mounted the buck-board.

"Up!" he called to the pair of bays and they started steadily but slowly. Now that Ramsey was going to get rid of a troublesome slave he was almost comfortable. His mind wandered. "In my day, if I or one of my brothers had used my father's best wagon for sparking, I would have been told off with a strap and so would any of my brothers."

Dudley Stark made no response. His mind was on the mental picture of that huge black slave seeing him for the first time in days.

"Strange to think that my boy will probably be married in a few years," Ramsey mused. "There's nothing wrong with being married (heavens, no!) but being single is so much more romantic. Every time in bed with a girl becomes an occasion of sin, and sin is exciting. Our churches have done a lot to make illicit romance exciting by calling it sinful. If our churches ever stop doing that, then a lot of fun will go out of the grandest game of all."

Dudley Stark paid his host the small compliment of giving a grunt in the way of response. He hadn't been listening to a word.

To their right, a wagon was in motion on the way back to the main house. It was too far away for Ramsey to make out the features of the girl with his son, but Dudley Stark couldn't help recognizing her. He gasped.

They drew up in front of the other wagon. Dudley heard his daughter's story about being knocked out and waking to find her horse was gone. If Dudley had any suspicions about her behavior, he kept them to himself.

Ramsey was rubbing the flame-red tip of his nose when he said, "Now that your daughter is here we can go ahead with our previous plan, Stark."

"The hanging, you mean?" Dudley Stark said grimly as his daughter gasped. "Yes, I want her to see it."

"Good. I'll get some rope near the fields and we'll have it done in almost no time." He glanced towards his son. "Follow Mr. Stark and myself, boy. And tell Miss Stark to bear up. I saw my first slave hanging when I was six years old, and my Grandfather Perley hoisted me on his shoulders so I could get a better sight of it. If you know that death isn't so far away from any of us, you'll be a better woman for it. 'In the midst of life, we are in death,' the Bible says, and you can't be too young to get the lesson driven home to you."

Dudley Stark asked irritably, "Can't we move this wagon?"

"Certainly." He raised his voice. "Colin, keep ten feet behind us. No less than ten."

Field slaves worked at their jobs with monotonous regularity. Their gestures were slow, their complaints numerous, and their faces looked as if all the life had been stamped out of them.

The overseer, dressed in white as Ramsey was, looked surprised by the interruption. Dudley Stark didn't like him at sight.

"Where's Ezekiel?" Ramsey asked, then, a little awkwardly, "You know who I mean."

"After what happened last night, Mr. Ramsey, you can be sure he's not at work." The overseer smiled. "He's over at the post."

"Let's go there. And bring enough rope."

The overseer didn't say anything to that, and he didn't seem surprised, either. He hurried over to where a slave group was bent over at their cotton picking, shouted at them to have finished a patch by the time he got back or he'd whip them all, and hurried back to the wagon. He was carrying strong gritty gray rope coiled carelessly and had to stop and make sure it didn't give. The chore took enough time so that Ramsey grew impatient.

"Finish that in the wagon," his boss shouted.

The overseer climbed in, fussing with the rope. "The

89

slave we want is prob'ly half-dead already by now. The rope won't have to work hard."

But it was nearly impossible for the overseer to keep the coiled rope together in a wagon pitching back and forth. It gave on him at least twice that Stark saw and he had to bend down frenziedly to draw the rope together. He was almost relieved when the wagon came in sight of the whipping post and he saw that it was empty and that as a result the pesky rope in this wagon might not have to be used for a while. But his smirk changed to a frown when he realized that the post ropes had been untied. A gray-haired Negro with a surprisingly youthful face was watching them, but he said nothing.

"Well?" Ramsey whirled on the overseer. "He's half-dead already, is he? He's at the post."

"I tied him there, myself, Mr. Ramsey," the overseer said feverishly. "Swear I did."

"You made a good job of it."

"Somebody else untied the knots."

The overseer, looking at the ground, said, "There are blood drops all over, you notice. Ezekiel couldn't have lived long with that much blood coming out of him. I'm plumb sure he's dead by now."

Ramsey, disappointed, looked across at Dudley Stark. "Couldn't be dead after a few little whiplashes, could he?"

"I don't believe it," Dudley said, determined not to believe it rather than because he had any reason to think that Hannibal was alive.

The overseer, trying to keep his job, said, "He probably started for the stream to cool himself off or wash away the blood, and died before he could get there. He may have been buried by one of the other boys in secrecy, but you can see for youself that the bloodstains stop all of a sudden. How could that happen if he hadn't died and the blood wasn't moving in his body any more?"

Ramsey pursed his lips. "Not a bad point."

90

Out of the corner of an eye, Dudley watched Leola and young Colin Ramsey step out of the other carriage. Upset as she was, there was a glow in Leola's face that Ramsey had never seen there before.

"I'll tell you one reason why there might not be blood drops on the earth after a certain point and the slave might still be alive," Dudley Stark said. "If he stole a horse and got on it, then there wouldn't be the drops on the ground."

Ramsey said briskly, "That's right! And your daughter did have a horse stolen from her."

The overseer smiled without pleasure. "Do you really think, Mr. Stark, that this here slave rode a horse out through Bon Repos and he wasn't seen?"

"He wasn't seen by any whites, or they'd have raised the alarm," Dudley insisted. He turned halfway around. "Put some pressure on that nigger over there and you'll find out if my Hannibal was seen."

Ramsey said, "No, I'd rather leave him alone."

Dudley Stark pointed out, "He's your only witness."

Leola's face had become papery white. Dudley Stark turned without permission and whistled toward the bland-looking young Negro.

"Come over here, boy," he shouted.

The youthful-faced Negro did, but he walked warily. A hand was raised to his face as if to defend himself.

"Boy, I want you to tell me—"

He got no further. The overseer chuckled and said, "Not a chance of that, Mr. Stark."

Dudley whirled on him. "The boy can hear what I say and he can see that I mean business."

At the sound of authority in another voice, the overseer looked respectful. "Well, this boy talked too much back at Mr. Ramsey a few years ago, and the overseer at that time was a little too anxious to show his authority, so this boy's tongue was cut out."

Dudley looked at the slave as if he wanted it confirmed. The slave opened his mouth. Dudley could see the mouth without a tongue except for part of a stump. He turned away.

"The boy can see and hear, Mr. Stark, like you said," the overseer went on, "but he can't talk."

"He can nod yes or no if he's asked a question."

"Yes, but he gets so nervous and flustered that you can't trust him to tell you anything except what he thinks you want to hear," the overseer said. "That boy is scared all the time, for some reason, and you can't believe a word he—well, you know. He's even more of a liar than the rest of them."

Ramsey said to the tongueless slave, "You can go, now."

Dudley felt sure that Leola's face showed considerable relief, but couldn't bring himself to look. The slave without a tongue was out of sight almost as soon as the words left Ramsey's mouth.

"I'm going out to look for Han—" Dudley stopped himself. "No, I think I'd best take my daughter home first. It'll save you people some inconvenience."

They rode home in Dudley's trap, with Leola pitching back and forth as it moved. Dudley, driving the team of horses, didn't look at his daughter any more than he thought was necessary.

"I want to know this one thing from you," he said. "Did you help that slave get away?"

"No, Daddy."

"Something else. Did anything happen between you and him before the getaway? Did he try and do anything to you?"

"No, Daddy, on my word he didn't. I never even saw him, I tell you."

Dudley judged that the horses could get along without direct supervision for a moment and took that much time to look across at his daughter.

"I'm going to find him and hang him, Leola," he said. "With my own bare hands if I have to. Do you understand?"

"Of course, Daddy, after what happened at Safe Harbor."

"Good. In the circumstances, I don't think that we should talk about it to your mother. She'd only suspect the worst, and I wouldn't want her to be worried and upset."

"Whatever you say, Daddy, is what I'll do," Leola said and meant it at the moment. "You know that."

But Dudley had underestimated Nettie, as it happened. He wanted to go out again and try to hunt down the missing Hannibal, but she cornered him before he could leave so quickly and unexpectedly. There was an argument between them, and Dudley had to tell what he knew before being able to leave the house without using violence on his dear wife.

Nettie sought out her daughter afterwards. Leola was trying to read a new book translated from the French of Mr. Victor Hugo. She put the book down gladly, wondering what she would look like in a gypsy costume like Esmeralda's in the novel, when her mother appeared. Nettie stood with arms akimbo.

"You told Daddy that nothing happened between you and that black man today?"

"It's the truth," Leola flared.

"Naturally I don't know whether it is or not, even though I've got my suspicions," Nettie said darkly. "There's only one thing I want you to do."

"Well?"

"Make sure that Daddy believes what you say," Nettie told her daughter quietly. "If not, and he gets upset about this, too, I swear I'll wring your neck."

93

She left without another word. Leola looked wonderingly after her. Each parent wanted to make sure that the other believed what was best. She supposed that the two of them were still in love after so many years of marriage. Then she dismissed them from her mind and wondered what Hannibal might be doing at this moment.

CHAPTER 10

The horse showed signs of tiredness. Hannibal got off and led her to water. When the horse was finished she still seemed tired. Hannibal wouldn't hold onto a tired horse, so he turned Darling around and slapped her on the rump and sent her back.

He wasn't so strange-looking now, a colored man on a horse. But he could be stopped by almost any white, and he'd be asked a lot of questions he might not be able to answer without giving himself away. If he was going to look like somebody who had always been free, then he'd have to look different in some way . . .

"Hey, you!" It was a white man on a white horse with brown spots at the nose. "What are you doing there?"

Hannibal looked from right to left, but couldn't get away before the man on the horse came closer. He was a small man, blond, with no brows and eyes the same color as water on a clear day. He carried a riding crop, and the horse would catch up to him more quickly than he could possibly run.

"You're a runaway, aren't you?" The riding crop was at his side. "Hungry?"

"I—I'm no runaway."

"Don't be silly. I wouldn't expect to see a free man without shoes or a shirt. Your skin is so black that it stands out against the trees. That's how I happened to see you."

There was nothing more to say. Hannibal shook with anger that he couldn't help.

"I'll tell you what we can do," the man said. "Are you up to walking?"

"Yes."

The white man didn't seem to notice Hannibal's disrespect in leaving out the word "sir."

"Walk in front of me," the white man said. "I'll tell you where to go in case there's any trouble. If somebody asks about you, then you're a new slave of mine. Tell me your name, so I'll know it."

"Joe," Hannibal said, telling a lie and being plainly disrespectful at the same time.

"Walk in front of me and the horse, Joe, and walk slowly. This won't take long."

Hannibal trudged down a dirt road toward what he was pretty sure would be life as a slave again. He turned left at the white man's softly spoken request.

A house came in view, not a big house like those at Bon Repos or Safe Harbor, but not a house with slave pens as any part of it, either.

"Wait outside, Joe," the white man said. "I can't ask you in or my wife would have my hide off me in little strips."

As if the likes of Hannibal would be asked into a house like that one! Who did the white man think he was fooling?

The white man rode off to stable his horse. Hannibal, deciding that he would try to run at the first sign of trouble, sat down to rest against a tree. The white man waved at him as he walked into the house.

Hannibal couldn't figure out how the white man was going to turn him in. With the white man in the house it was possible to run out the same way he had come in.

The white man suddenly stuck his head out of a window and called, "Stand up, Joe."

Hannibal, planning to run, stood. The man looked him up and down, then nodded a couple of times.

"You're almost as big as this house," he said, then pulled

96

his head back in. It didn't take longer than a deep breath of relief on Hannibal's part before the man had stuck his head out the window again. "You can sit down now."

It was upsetting to be looked at when he didn't expect it. Hannibal finally decided that he would sit down so he could rest as long as possible; but as soon as the front door opened again he would run.

When the door opened and the white man appeared, though, he was carrying a blue shirt in one hand a pair of shoes in the other. Hannibal stood, fascinated.

"Here's a shirt that I think will fit," he said. "I'm not certain about the shoes, but I simply took the biggest pair I could find."

The shirt fit better than Hannibal would have expected. There was a stocking inside each shoe, and Hannibal couldn't get them on the way they ought to have fit, according to the white man. As for the shoes themselves, they pinched his toes badly. Hannibal had never worn a pair of shoes before in his life and he stared down at himself as if he couldn't believe what he was seeing.

"A pair of shoes you've never worn before always hurts you right away," the white man said as if Hannibal ought to have known that. "You always get used to them after you've tied the laces."

Hannibal nodded and looked away, rather than thanking a white man for a favor.

"Something else, Joe," the white man said. "I can take you to a man who makes a specialty of smuggling slaves up to the North. Be a lot easier for you than trying to get up North by yourself, you know."

"I don't want to go any way except by myself," Hannibal said firmly, remembering Sam Rinders. "Please, no."

"If you walk through the southern states, you'll have a hard time persuading people you're a free darkie," the white man said. "Wait a minute, though. Maybe I can help you with that."

97

Hannibal waited, feeling his toes almost doubled up on themselves and against the bottoms of his feet. When he made a move his face would crumple with pain.

The white man got back with two sheets of paper in a hand. He waved them toward Hannibal.

"Can you read? Well, it won't make much difference. This yellow paper is an identification. It says that your name is Homer. The white paper is something I just wrote up. It says that the slave, Homer, is a free man. It's signed by Breckenridge Holloman, who was Homer's owner. Holloman passed away not long ago, leaving no estate to speak of. I took Homer and tried to set him free, but he said he would be too scared of that. He was here until one of the horses stomped him to death a few weeks ago."

Hannibal nodded, although his eyes were glued to the yellow paper and the white one.

"If somebody important asks who you are and wants you to prove it, you just pull out these two papers. Understand?"

"Yes. Yes." Hannibal took the papers tenderly and eased them into a pocket.

"Good luck," the white man said. "I mean that, you know."

"Thank you."

The white man looked up and down to make sure nobody was in sight. Only then did he smile and draw out a hand.

"Let's shake on it," he said.

Hannibal was nervous about doing it, but the hand was just ordinary and not really much different from his own. Except for the color of the skin, of course.

He had figured on walking around the next town, once he got close to it. He had never been inside a town, though, except for riding through one when he had been sold. He had never walked in a town and it seemed like a sign for him that new times had come.

He was uncomfortable from the start and kept turning nervously from left to right. Never before had he seen so many people. They walked on wooden boards that had been put up above mud and dirt and horse leavings. There were little places where other whites sold things, and even a man who cut hair for money. Whites stood and talked to each other and smiled and were at ease. The only blacks he saw were two men in front of carriages. The men stared at him until his eyes met theirs, and then they looked in a different direction.

The shoes still hurt, though, and he decided to take them off. Should anybody want to know, he'd be able to prove he was free just by showing two pieces of paper. It didn't make any difference if he wore shoes or not.

There was a round place between two facing rows of wooden boards. The round place was just about filled with water, but it was possible to sit at the edges. A pair of whites were doing it.

Hannibal sat down at the far end and pulled off one of the shoes. He was working his toes and starting to pull off the other one when he saw a pair of shadows on each side of him. The two white men had stood up and come over to face him. One was small and thin, the other man big and burly with a deep tan and handlebar mustaches.

"What are you doing here, boy?"

"I'm passing through," Hannibal said, and then drew a deep breath. "And I'm not a boy."

"You're at a white man's fountain," the small one said. "No niggers allowed over here."

"Don't you call me—"

"We'll call you anything we want, boy," the burly man said. "You a runaway?"

"I'm free."

"Prove it." The small man smiled nastily when Han-

99

nibal didn't make a move and added, "Do you want to get thrown in jail around here, boy? I'm the town constable."

Hannibal wanted to ask him to prove that, but figured that the white man would call other whites to look at him for being so uppity and he'd find himself in that much more trouble. He drew out the precious papers and started to hand them across, but unfolded them at the last moment and showed them that way.

"If you even put one finger on this, constable or not," Hannibal said quietly, "you'll never put a finger on nothing else ever again."

The small man suddenly laughed instead of getting mad. "It's upside down, nigger."

"I told you not to call me that."

"It's what you are, isn't it? That's like my asking people not to say I'm short. Turn your paper so that the bottom side is on top."

Hannibal did it. The constable, if that was what he happened to be, didn't lean forward to look at it. Instead he asked quietly, "What's your name?"

"Homer."

The small man turned toward the bigger one. "I guess he's free and he's proved his point, so you wouldn't be doing any damage to somebody's property."

Before Hannibal could make any other move, the burly white man with the handlebar mustaches suddenly pulled out a hard heavy hand which sent Hannibal reeling backwards and into the warm and dirty water.

Hannibal couldn't thrash around because he wanted to keep the papers dry, so he kept going under. He would come up for a breath and then sink down again. He finally found out that he could be quiet in the water, just laying there, and he wouldn't go down. Outside and around him, though, he could hear white people laughing at him.

(If he had still been a slave, none of this would have

100

happened. But he would have been hanged by Master Dudley Stark, though. It was better to remember that whenever he started to feel sorry for himself.)

Keeping the papers dry, he suddenly doubled his legs under him. They touched solid ground, and he was able to stand up in the water. Except for the papers, he was soaked to the skin.

He was walking carefully as he stepped out of the fountain. The crowd of whites looked at him as if they couldn't make up their minds to be fascinated by him or disgusted.

The small man said, "This nigger decided to go swimming in your fountain, which shows you what he thinks of you and everybody else in this town."

Somebody else shouted, "Send him back where he belongs. He's a runaway."

"Now friends, let us be fair," the small man said just as Hannibal was becoming scared he had been found out. "This man is a free nigger, and the papers he carries with him are the proof of it."

Some men in the audience looked disappointed. It was a woman who called, "String him up!"

A man echoed, "That's right, string him up! Learn him with a rope!"

"Now friends, there's no need to use a rope," the small man said. "A rope teaches no man anything. But we can indeed teach this nigger how to behave toward whites as long as the town has a visitor who is willing to stand up and be its champion. I'm referring to Felix Quayle over here."

The big man suddenly raised both hands in a fist over his head. Some men in the audience cheered and a few of them clapped hands.

"If you want to see Felix Quayle teach this boy a lesson he'll never forget, then come to the Meadow tonight. Bring your wives and children for this edifying spectacle. I may add that Felix Quayle will fight any town cham-

101

pion, any *man*, who is willing to stay in the ring with him for three rounds. Or is able to do so. Come one, come all, to the Meadow tonight."

The small man said a few more words, and then the crowd started to thin out. The people glared at Hannibal as they broke up, and in most cases he glared back. There was a clear path to the far end of town, the other end from which he had come, and he started for it. Nobody stopped him until he was far away from the fountain and then he was stopped by a colored gal who purposely walked in front of him.

The gal was a head shorter than Hannibal. She had a little squib of a nose and eyes that were never still. She smiled at him as if they were old friends.

She said to him, "Let's go where it's quiet."

He stared at her. She didn't look like the sort of gal who had to sell herself to make money.

She was pretty and she smelled good, though. Maybe he would go with her and she would give him what he had just made up his mind he wanted.

She said, "I've got a room in the only boarding place in town that would take us. You come with me and if nothing else I'll dry you out in no time."

He put up a hand in front of his face to keep from smiling, even though he didn't like it when gals talked dirty.

"I need to get dried out," he said.

"Are you all right otherwise?"

"No sickness."

She didn't pay attention to that, but said, "Come with me."

The boarding house was almost the same kind of shanty as the slave pens. The gal had a room to herself, though. There was a double bed and a mirror, and a few chairs.

"Take your clothes off," the gal said. "Get into bed and cover yourself."

"Sure." This was going to be much easier than Han-

102

nibal had expected. He took off the soggy clothes and draped them across a chair in the best way he could.

"First of all, we ought to arrange about the money," she said, smiling.

Hannibal started to clear his throat before explaining that he didn't have any. He might say that he had lost it in the water and even make a point of looking for it in those wet pants pockets.

The gal drew out a bill, though, and passed it across to him and said:

"Here you are, for your trouble."

He reached for it and put it next to the papers which he had set down on the bed.

"You're paying *me?*" he asked, dazed, then suddenly pulled the cover more closely around him. "What do you want? What kind of a gal are you?"

"I told you I'm going to dry you out," she murmured, picking up his clothes and setting them across three washboards on the iron rim of a tub. "In an hour or so, you'll be ready."

"I thought you were—well, you know."

"I'm not, thanks to Felix."

"You mean Quayle? That white bastard who gave me such a hard time?"

"He gave you a hard time, but you're getting paid for it," the gal said. "I waited for you to start moving away and then I came with the money. It's part of Felix's work."

"What kind of work is it when you push poor niggers around like he does?"

"Felix fights from town to town for his money," she said. "Him and Porky, his manager, always start something with one of ours in a new town. The whites watch and they say they want to come to the fight just to see one of ours get whipped real good."

"Am I supposed to fight with him? Is that what the money is for?"

"Better don't go near the place," the gal said. "A white

103

crowd really hates to see one of ours in the ring with a white man. Besides, Porky can say from the ring that you ran away instead of fighting and the crowd applauds."

Hannibal shuddered, then looked up at her. "And you're Felix Quayle's fancy gal?"

She shrugged. "It's better than being in a whorehouse and it's a lot better than being a maid. I know what I'm saying. I've tried both."

"Is he rough on you?"

"Felix? No. He does his fighting in the ring." She threw her head back and laughed. "Don't forget something else. He has to be in good shape to fight, and when he's been with me he's only in shape to sleep and he goes through the next day feeling groggy. So he don't come around as often as other men might."

"What's your name?"

"Cindy. And you?"

"Call me either Homer or Joe or Hannibal."

She said, "I guess Hannibal is right. You look more like a Hannibal than a Joe or a Homer."

Hannibal patted the bed space beside him. "Come over and sit near me."

"All right," Cindy said surprisingly, but sat down on a chair near the bed. "Is this close enough?"

"No. But I won't touch you unless you want me to, when you get closer."

"I wouldn't want you to."

"Then I wouldn't touch."

"I'd just be getting you all bothered for no reason," Cindy said carefully. "Nothing would come of it."

"When is the last time you were with one of ours?" he asked, suddenly curious. "Can you remember?"

"That time was worse than anything with Felix, but I won't tell you about it," she said. "Felix gets his meanness out in the ring, you know. Boxers make good boyfriends."

She sat down on the bed, but wouldn't face him. All the same he reached up and touched her breasts through the cloth and squeezed them lightly.

"I told you not to—"

"Well, I'm not sure just yet if you really want me to or you don't," Hannibal said carefully.

"Damn you," Hannibal, I won't let anything like it happen. I've had enough of poor lazy niggers in my time. Can't work or hate to, and resent you because you can make more money than them. It doesn't pay."

"I'm not lazy."

"Not with your hands you aren't," she agreed.

"Not at all I'm not," he insisted. "You show me the way to get money and I'll do it."

She asked slyly, "You'd go into the ring with Felix?"

"If I could get money for it, that's just what I'd do."

"He's a dirty fighter, and he's been at it long enough to know every trick there is, but he pays people who go three rounds with him."

"He pays money for somebody who fights him, so I'll do it, Cindy, for sure."

She was concerned, though. A frown had appeared on her face. "You can't let yourself get killed! A nigger coming up there will get himself done forever."

"Then at least I'll go out fighting." Hannibal grinned. "But I'll be all right. It's at the Meadow tonight, and I'll find the place."

"No, I won't let you." She had come closer. "I'll keep you here and you'll be too tired to fight."

Hannibal threw his head back and laughed. "I can take care of him in one way and you in another. Want to bet?"

And he reached for her, bending her head down towards his. She returned his fierce kiss, but her fists lashed out and hit him at the sides. Hannibal, letting her try to pummel him, undid her dress and the yards of frilly clothes under it. As her body wouldn't move from the

105

top of his, he simply reached down and stretched out her legs, then spread them.

He hadn't expected anything more than a tumble in the hay with another girl, but the way it happened was a little different. Not that either of them did any new things to the other, but only that he felt as if he wanted to keep her with him forever. He touched her small breasts gently instead of mashing them as he sometimes did, for example. It was Cindy who pulled his hand toward the breasts, wanting him to squeeze harder.

When it had happened at last, and each was satisfied, she swiftly said, "Again."

Hannibal smiled and did his part with pleasure. This time as they were finished he stroked her hair as she kissed him lightly.

She said urgently, "Again!"

Hannibal kept smiling, but he shook his head this time. "I wouldn't mind at any other time, but three trips to the well are too much for a man who has to do some fighting in a little while."

"Hannibal, I won't let you go out there and get killed!" she protested.

His smile was serene. "I'm going to get some sleep, Cindy. Believe me, I'll be up before dark."

"Hannibal, you're the biggest fool that God ever made, and He made some beauties."

He eased her body down till she was next to him on the bed. "We sleep together, Cindy. Sleeping alone is downright bad for the health."

CHAPTER 11

"If anybody wants to test his skills in the fistic arts and thinks that he can last three rounds with one of the greatest boxers of all time, let him stand up and come to the front of the crowd."

People looked around to see who was taking the challenge. In the rear, Hannibal stood up from a wooden chair and walked to the end of the row and then downwards. It surprised him that nobody had called out when he started to move, but he supposed that people couldn't see the color of his skin in the darkness.

And then he understood why he had hardly been noticed. A dim shape was moving in front of him toward the ring, as well. Hannibal could have put on a burst of speed and got to the ring first, but he decided to let Felix Quayle get a little tired before fighting him.

The Meadow was a stretch of flat country, and a square ring had been set down on it for the occasion, complete with a double set of ropes on each side. There were some empty seats, but not a woman or a child was in sight.

The white challenger had stepped into the ring and was looking around sheepishly at the torchlights in each corner. The manager, the small and thin man who was called Porky for some reason or other, raised both hands for silence.

"A brave soul has appeared at last," he said, then smiled at the audience. "There was a nigger in town who was invited, but I guess he got himself a case of the nigger

107

disease: scaredness." The audience laughed. "There's another nigger disease I guess you all know about, but I won't mention it right here."

The words drew another long laugh and a scattering of applause. Hannibal, who had taken the nearest empty seat, found himself sitting on the edge of it.

"Your name, please? Talk a little louder, if you don't mind. There's nothing to be worried about just yet. . . . Jim Izzard? All right, Jim. You know the rules of this sporting contest?"

Jim Izzard nodded. Probably he couldn't trust himself to say anything.

"All right, Jim. You know that I can't do anything in case the worst happens when you're in the ring with Felix Quayle. Once you're alone with him, you're on your own. Is that understood, Jim? It is? Okay."

The manager hesitated. Quayle, having sized up the other man, was running both thumbnails along his handlebar mustaches while he waited.

"Do you have any illnesses, Jimmy? Heart okay? Lungs? Ever had your appendix taken out? Ever get the vapors? No to everything, huh, Jimmy? Then I guess you'll do. Strip to the waist, Jimmy, and we'll get this sporting contest under way."

There were some shouts and cheers for Jimmy and an occasional reverse cheer. Somebody shouted at him:

"There's only one bed in the hospital, so you'd better hurry up and fill it."

Both men faced each other in pants and shoes. They would be fighting bare-knuckle, which was good news to Hannibal; he had never fought any other way. The two men shook hands. Felix Quayle looked so much bigger than the other fighter that it was hard to keep from being sorry for the local boy. Jimmy Izzard winced and called out, then rubbed his hand. Felix Quayle had done his first dirty trick of the night.

108

"When the bell rings you'll come out fighting, and you'll rest at the next ring," Porky shouted.

In the pause while the two men waited for the bell to ring, Hannibal had time to wish he hadn't been so anxious to make love to Cindy. He was feeling just a bit lazy, with some of the fine edge honed off.

Cindy had come out here with him, talking all the time in hopes of persuading him against making the fight. Hannibal had finally moved away from her when they reached the Meadow. He felt sure she was in the crowd and wished she was next to him at the moment in spite of all her jabbering.

The fight started. Hannibal, having expected he would enjoy seeing two whites cut each other to pieces, realized he was only going to see one white cut up. And it would be the wrong one, at that.

Quayle was giving the other man a chance to look good for his neighbors, and was carrying him in order to do it. Jimmy Izzard didn't know the first thing about punching, so he missed a few good chances. Quayle came close, allowed Izzard to get in an occasional off-center punch and made it look stronger than it had been by falling back. Before Izzard would get to him, Quayle would make believe he had lost his balance and got it back just in time. Quayle was actually fighting for two people, but he must have done it often enough in his time and he was pretty good at it.

Izzard was suffering from the hurt hand, but it wouldn't have made much difference. He simply wasn't much of a fighter.

The round was over and on three sides of him people said that they sure hadn't figured old Jimmy Izzard to go this far with a real fighter and come out of it looking so good.

"It's not over yet," one of them said darkly. "A boxer gets his wind after the first few rounds."

109

"I'll bet you a quarter Jimmy Izzard is on his feet after the third round."

"I think you're probably right, but it sounds like a good bet anyhow. I'll take it."

The bell rang for round number two. Izzard moved forward too quickly, hurting his elbow against Quayle's chest. He stood groggy with pain. Quayle may have wanted to keep the audience interested for a little longer, but he had to move in and give Izzard a pair of punches. Izzard was carried out of the ring by two of his friends.

There was a scattering of applause for the challenger, and somebody near Hannibal murmured that the elbow punch hadn't been fair.

Porky, the manager, stood in the ring beside Quayle, who didn't even look winded.

"Is there any other brave man in the audience, a man who is willing to take his life in his hands and try to go three rounds with this great fighter? Three rounds for a purse of ten dollars. That amounts to three dollars and thirty-three and one-third cents for each and every round, gentlemen. Anybody in the audience? Anybody at all?"

Hannibal made his move, getting to his feet, and walked toward the ring. The manager, squinting into near-darkness, smiled and waved.

"We have another challenger right here, gents, a man who doesn't care what happened to another man not that long ago, a true sportsman who is determined——"

He stopped himself. His jaw snapped shut.

Finally he said, "Felix Quayle don't fight niggers."

Hannibal had already leaped up to the outside of the ring, on the slim end of the rope boundary.

"You said I was too scared to show up, but I'm not," he snapped. "If your boy don't want to fight, then we know who's really scared."

Porky shouted angrily, "Mr. Quayle wouldn't get his hands dirty on a nigger!"

110

He had never talked so loudly, it seemed, but people close by were shouting back.

"Let him get his brains beaten."

"I haven't seen a nigger take a whipping in years."

And somebody else, calling directly to the person who'd said that: "Yes, but not with the fists."

"The nig won't even last one round."

"That's right. Quayle took it easy on Jimmy, but he's a sure bet to kill the nigger."

Quayle had drawn back very slightly, wanting to examine Hannibal. He looked carefully, not seeming bored now or taking the time to preen his mustaches.

"We'll put it to a vote," Porky said. "All those in favor of this nigger getting into a ring with a white man, say 'Aye' . . . all those against say 'Nay' . . ."

The nay chorus was distinctly weaker, but Porky said, "The nays have it. Now is there a *man* who . . . ?"

But a chorus of jeers had gone up.

"Let's see if Quayle can kill himself a nigger."

"Give it to the nigger."

"Let's see how Quayle fights for real."

Hannibal knew he would never have been allowed to go near the ring if it had been considered that he might win. He may have looked calm on the outside, but inwardly his pulses were racing as never before. He entered the ring.

Carefully he took off his shirt, then hesitated and took his shoes off, too. There was a mild laugh in the audience when he did that, but Hannibal knew he'd be better off in the ring without the pesky things.

"Our African friend wants to be more comfortable," Porky said sarcastically. "Our African *monkey* friend, I ought to be saying."

Hannibal didn't make any response except for showing a fist that moved gently in the manager's direction. Porky swallowed once, shot a glance at Felix Quayle and then turned back to the audience.

111

"I'll tell you how we work it," Porky said. "Wait until the bell rings and come out fighting. Stop when the bell rings again. Fight for three periods. If you can get out of the ring on your own power after three rounds, you'll win ten dollars. Now I want you to face Mr. Quayle over there."

Hannibal hadn't moved. He asked, "Who's going to hold the ten dollars? I don't trust you."

There was some laughter in the audience. Nobody said a word, and it began to look as if the crowd would be cheated of their sport. A man stood up and raised his hands to the corners of his lips.

He called out, "I'll hold it, nigger."

Somebody else shouted, "Who's gonna hold you?"

Hannibal nodded his approval, on the notion that one local white man was as good as another. Nobody saw his nod, nor did it change any responses.

"Very well," Porky decided, "just to quiet our suspicious African friend over here."

He counted out the money and put it into an envelope, then made a point of leaving the ring and bringing the envelope over toward the man. Along the way he dropped it, but picked it up promptly.

Back in the ring, where the two fighters glared at each other, Porky coughed and cleared his throat before turning to the audience again.

"We can't expect our African friend here to know the Marquis of Queensberry rules," he began, and paused for the mild laugh that had been sure to follow. "As a result, and except for the business of keeping rounds, this fight will be in a catch-as-catch-can style. Anything goes. The only rule except for the one about the rounds is that there aren't going to be any rules."

Wild applause broke out once again. Hannibal saw Porky catch Felix Quayle's eye and wink once. He looked around quickly as if to find the trap right away, but it wasn't in sight.

112

Porky said, "Now shake hands with him, Felix, and come out fighting."

Hannibal moved toward Quayle, who promptly stepped on his naked feet. Hannibal nearly called out and actually drew up his fists, but Quayle stepped back and the manager stepped between them, both hands toward Hannibal.

"We start when the bell goes and not before," he said sternly.

Hannibal would have chased Quayle, but his feet hurt so blindingly he couldn't do it, let alone make himself move. He stayed in place, though, wanting Quayle to come to him for the handshake and determined to get one hand in a grip that the white man would never forget.

Quayle got the better of him again, though, not coming a step closer and talking so that the people in the crowd could hear what he said.

"I won't shake hands with a nigger," he told them all.

Somebody in the crowd cheered him, and there was a murmur of approval.

The manager droned, "When the bell rings you start to fight and when it rings again you stop fighting. Now!"

He walked over to the edge of the ring, eased himself through the ropes and dropped out of sight. A bell rang and the fight was on.

Quayle must have known how hard it would be for Hannibal to move, but stood off to one side and waited for Hannibal to hurt his feet by coming closer. Hannibal wouldn't do that, though. Instead he watched Quayle move around the ring and himself moved so as to face him. It hurt to move that way, too, but not as much as the start of fighting could have done.

"What is this?" one of the customers called out.

"It's a dance, that's what."

"A co-till-eeon."

"Can I have the next waltz?"

Quayle was angry now, and he was a man who could be deadly in anger. He had to come in toward Hannibal, and each of them knew it. He moved swiftly, a hand raised as if to throw it. Hannibal ducked that and nearly stepped into a hard right. It grazed his chin, but even the closeness of it made him dizzy and he nearly lost his balance.

Quayle didn't need any more of an invitation, but moved in swiftly to finish the fight. Hannibal let him come close and then struck, landing a solid punch to the chest among the three that he lashed out with. Quayle staggered back, but caught himself.

The audience was jeering him, now.

"Can't even fight a nigger."

"Let him have the right, Quayle, the right!"

Quayle came in again, but was met by a flurry of punches that sent him back. He did manage to land one just beneath Hannibal's eye, but it wasn't going to change the course of the fight no matter how it went from there.

All the same, the crowd seemed to think he had done something worthwhile.

"Nigger's gonna get him a white eye," a man called.

"That nigger punches even worse than other niggers."

"Anybody want to bet on him?"

"Not him."

"Come on, Vic, you've got the ten bucks. Raise the stake with a bet."

The pain in Hannibal's feet was less and he met Quayle more than halfway when the boxer came toward him again. Hannibal aimed for the lips, wanting to wipe that smirk off his face and wanting everybody to know that the damage had been done by a man of his race.

He left himself wide open for a punch to the heart, though, and it knocked the breath out of him. Quayle was punching him on the sides with each hand. Hannibal fell back against the ropes, which shook when his body fell against them. With his right hand he punched Quayle just above the bridge of the nose. It was an accident because he had wanted to give Quayle a swollen eye instead.

The punch didn't mark Quayle, but it sent him staggering back and reeling. He was keeping his feet with difficulty, and they might have buckled at any moment. The crowd was jeering him.

The bell rang, and the manager appeared in center ring and took his fighter off to one side. A small chair appeared and Quayle took it. The manager poured water on Quayle's face. Hannibal watched, resting against the ropes. There wasn't anybody who would help him.

Somebody called, "Give the nig a chair for between rounds, at least."

"If he sits down, he'll fall asleep, just like the rest of 'em."

"He ain't been sleeping out there."

"He ain't been winning, either."

Hannibal stood, eyes closed, face set. He had rested like this sometimes in the fields. Instead of hot sun, there was the warmth of torchlight near him. He tried to keep from remembering Miriam's voice and her face and the touch of her body when she was close.

"What's that runt waiting for?" a man in the crowd asked. "Let him start the next round."

"I didn't think the jig would last this long."

"He's probably cheating, that jig. Don't forget, in this fight anything goes."

Porky had disappeared and the small wooden chair was gone from Quayle's corner. Quayle stood up. He didn't look as sure of himself as before. His handlebar mustaches drooped at the corners.

The bell rang to start the next round. Quayle ran out, but Hannibal walked slowly. The crowd jeered him for that, but he couldn't have cared less. The crowd would jeer him for whatever he did, and it came to him for the first time that they might do him some harm if he won. At this moment, he didn't care.

Quayle made contact right away, using one hand to cover his punch below the belt. Hannibal doubled up, and Quayle punched him in the face. It straightened Hannibal out for the flurry of punches that was to come. Hannibal fell against the ropes, raised one foot and pushed Quayle halfway across the ring.

Somebody shouted, "What the hell kind of a fight is this, anyhow?"

"What do you expect with a jig?"

Somebody else shouted, "No rules, remember? Anything goes here."

Quayle was coming back towards him, but this time Hannibal was ready. He punched as hard as he could, aiming for Quayle's stomach. He didn't know how many punches he landed, but Quayle suddenly doubled up and his face was where the top of his stomach had been. The chance was too good to miss. Hannibal started to hit out again, but realized he had been hit hard and below the belt when his mind was on the damage he was going to do.

Hannibal let out a gasp and reeled. No bell was heard in time to save him. He could do nothing except run from Quayle till he was stronger.

The audience jeered him, of course, but he had got used to that and it didn't make any impression on him.

"Catch him by the toe," somebody called out. "That's where you always catch one of them."

"If it was a race, he'd win."

"Give him a wagon."

Hannibal stopped himself, driven by desperation. The round wouldn't finish until Quayle got into trouble again, so Hannibal had to get Quayle in trouble as fast as possible.

Quayle, coming closer, made as if to punch. Actually he raised a foot and plunged it toward Hannibal's right kneecap. Hannibal had seen the move coming. He

116

stepped to one side, and punched the professional fighter in the center of the stomach. Quayle gasped, and his face became gray. With his last strength, Hannibal closed in for what he hoped might end the fight.

Somebody shouted, "Ring the goddam bell."

The bell rang, finishing the round. Hannibal staggered to the opposite corner from Quayle, who was being attended by the manager once more. A customer had carried his wooden chair up to the ring and eased it through the ropes so Hannibal would have a place to rest between rounds.

"What did you do that for?" somebody complained.

"Aw, it didn't seem right that one of 'em should get some help and the nigger get nothing."

"You a jig-lover or what?"

"No, no, 'course not." A pause. "Well, I figured that if one of 'em sits down he won't get himself to stand again. Next time Quayle is sure gonna kill him."

"That's more like a good reason."

Hannibal sat with eyes closed, feeling the pains all over him. The trouble with resting up was simply that you had more chances to feel the pain.

This pause lasted longer than the first one, which was a sure sign that things hadn't been too easy for Felix Quayle, either. There was considerable pleasure in knowing that as long as he was in this square ring he was able to raise his fists to a white man and nobody outside was going to punish him for it.

When he opened his eyes he was alone with Quayle in this ring, the professional fighter standing because his chair had been taken away. He started to use the ropes as if they were a pair of oars in a boat, but the ring had been built badly and the ropes and the wood seemed to shake when he tried that.

There was a hubbub in the audience. Somebody said, "Even in this fight, that wouldn't be decent."

"The only rule in this fight is about keeping to rounds. Nothing else makes a difference."

"Well, I don't like it."

"Nothing'll happen 'less the jig cheats Quayle and gets him in a mess."

"One thing I tell you: he'd better not leave the jig on his feet again after this round because he loses the ten dollars and he'll never fight here again."

"That's right. Anybody who's too tenderhearted to take a jig simply don't belong in Alabama."

"So we're all agreed 'bout—you know?"

"I guess."

The bell rang for the third and last round.

Quayle came charging out of his corner and Hannibal stood up slowly. As he walked out he flexed his fingers in trying to get some power back into them.

Quayle got to him first with a body blow and followed it up with a punch that landed just below Hannibal's neck. Hannibal felt the man's knee against his foot and then raised his own knee. It hit Quayle in the crotch. He let out a scream almost like a woman and feel away, holding his crotch. He fell against the ropes, which nearly collapsed at the weight and dragged the wooden posts down with them.

He turned toward the audience, though, instead of trying to protect himself against a sudden rush. Hannibal started toward him at full speed, though, intending to pummel Felix Quayle and knock him down.

Because he was running he was in time to see the black object fly through the air and land at Quayle's feet. Quayle ducked down for it. The object crackled in the air as he straightened himself. It was a riding crop.

The audience cheered and laughed and applauded.

"Now he'll get what he deserves."

"He's been begging for this."

"It's about time!"

Quayle drew up the riding crop and lashed Hannibal

once with it, across the right shoulder. It drew blood and made a cruel-looking welt.

The crowd cheered. The look of furious pleasure in Quayle's face was enough to prove to Hannibal that the professional fighter was intending to commit murder.

Quayle certainly was carrying a murder weapon, but he couldn't use it without pulling his hand back to make a half-circle in order to get any play with the riding crop. In that time he would be defenseless. He wasn't dealing with a slave who had to endure punishment on pain of being killed.

Hannibal waited till one brawny white arm was drawn back and then he charged into Felix Quayle.

All he wanted to do was to hit out at the man, but it wasn't that simple. Quayle was already against the ropes. The weight of both of them against the ropes sent the posts tumbling down to the ring's edges. The ropes were flabby and crumpled. Layers of dust rose in the air.

Quayle was too close to get any effective play with the whip. Its tip hummed in the air, but it landed well away from Hannibal. Hannibal was using his fists. A punch to the jawline sent Quayle down. Even in this position he would be able to use the riding crop after a fashion. He was near an edge of the ring and he could draw the crop downwards and back in the air.

Hannibal raised a foot to kick the crop out of Quayle's hand. He suddenly slipped on the rope and fell almost on top of Quayle.

"Nigger bastard," the fighter gasped. "I'll kill you for this!"

Hannibal decided to keep Quayle still rather than fight him actively just then. He looped a section of rope around Quayle's neck. With one hand on the loop's end, he tightened it slightly to prove how much he could tighten it if he wanted to and maybe keep Quayle more calm.

119

Carefully he reached for the whip. Quayle wouldn't let go, but used his feet and hands as best he could.

The crowd was on its feet, now, and screaming at Hannibal. Somebody threw a chair, but it missed Hannibal. Other chairs were thrown, but they didn't reach him, either.

"Let's get the dam jig before he does some real harm to Quayle."

The harm had already been done, but by Quayle himself. Stretching to get the riding crop away from Hannibal he suddenly lost balance and tumbled over the ring's edge. With a hand on the loop, Hannibal knew what might happen. He let the loop go, but not before he had heard a cracking sound that he never wanted to hear again as long as he lived.

"The nigger hanged him," somebody shouted.

Hannibal darted to his feet.

A man called out, "Five dollars to the first man who kills him a nigger tonight."

There was a shot. Hannibal reeled, certain he had been hit and confused because he wasn't feeling the pain. He decided to fall. Only by making believe he was dead would he be likely to get out of here in one piece after awhile.

"You ain't hurt, Hannibal," said Cindy's voice from the ringside. "You come down from there and anybody who touches you will get hurt real bad. I've used guns before and I don't mind doing it again. I always bring a pistol with me to the fights."

CHAPTER 12

"The reason I carry a pistol," Cindy was saying quietly, almost as if there had been no break in the talk, "is that I've gotten Quayle out of dangerous spots from time to time. For instance, if he forgot himself and rammed some local fighter real good and the other locals wanted to come after him. Men are a lot more scared of a woman with a pistol than they might be if another man was carrying one, and especially a Negro woman."

They were at Cindy's boarding house. Cindy had gone back there with Hannibal, and they had spent what was left of the night together. Cindy insisted there was nothing to worry about, as she would keep the gun close to her. She put it under her pillow, but Hannibal was so worried that she put it under the bed. He was still shaky when they made love and it was harder for him to do than he could ever remember. When it was finished she picked up the pistol from under the bed, told him that the safety catch was on, and put it under her pillow. For once, he didn't even kiss her goodnight, not wanting to jar the pistol just in case.

Cindy packed her things swiftly. Like Hannibal, she knew it would be impossible to stay in this town. When she left the room to tell the landlady she was going and to order a wagon, Hannibal became moody. He couldn't help being sullen when she got back to the room and went on with the packing.

"What's wrong with you, Hannibal? You haven't said a word since heaven-knows-when."

"I was thinking that I can't go with you."

"For the Lord's sweet sake, Hannibal! Why ever not?"

"There are whites after me. A fellow who used to own me and who swears he'll hang me for messing with his daughter, although the gal wanted it even more than I did."

"Well, they're looking for you by yourself, and not for you with a gal," Cindy pointed out. "That makes a difference."

Hannibal looked down. "I've got no big money. I can't pay for nothing."

"You'll owe it to me and when you make some money you'll pay back every cent. I'll hound you until you pay back what you owe."

"I don't want you to carry me."

It was a stand-off. Cindy turned to the packing again, but only because she expected the man with the wagon to come by for them in a short time. She hadn't given up.

"You want us to be together, but you don't want me to do anything for us." She sniffed. "That's nigger thinking, for sure, boy. The stuff you've got on your skin won't never come off, even if it wasn't in your head, too."

Hannibal was going to say that he didn't understand what she was talking about. There was a light knock on the door. Cindy stopped in mid-motion, reached under the pillow for her pistol, and turned to the door.

"Who is it?"

"Mrs. Meek. The landlady."

Cindy glanced out the window, then frowned. "What is it, Mrs. Meek? The wagon hasn't come to take me out of here, just yet. At least, not as far as I can see."

"There's somebody to talk to you." The landlady gulped. "A man."

Cindy looked startled, as Hannibal could well understand. She had told him a while back that she didn't know any colored people in this town.

"One of ours?" she asked.

"No."

"Ask him to come up here. I've got a friend with me, and we'll leave the door open. Nothing will happen to him."

The landlady shuffled away. Cindy finished the last of her packing, then sat down on the double bed. She was holding the pistol at one side. Hannibal stood up and put his pants on.

A man's footsteps went decisively up the wooden stairs. He knocked at their door.

She called out, "Come in, Porky." With a glance at Hannibal she said, "It couldn't be anybody else."

But it wasn't Quayle's manager who walked into the small room. It was a well-dressed white man in riding boots, narrow pants and a thick shirt. The smell of horse came into the room with him. He was a tall man, gray at the temples. He was obviously a rich man because he was able to afford to protect himself from the sun as well as ride for pleasure. He gave the impression of a man who wanted to be more at ease outdoors than in a drawing room, but he would never get to that point.

He glanced down at the pistol, and his generous lips grew thin. "That won't be necessary."

"I hope not, sir," Cindy said, holding the pistol raised but not aimed directly at the visitor.

"I'm glad you know enough not to aim one of those infernal things unless you plan to shoot it."

"I do, sir. And I can pull off a snap shot, if I have to."

"It won't be necessary, now." He surprised Cindy and Hannibal by shutting the door firmly.

"I'd rather not be seen here if it isn't necessary," he said, and turned to Hannibal. "I see that you and your woman are planning to leave the neighborhood. That's very sensible."

Hannibal nodded, but didn't say anything.

"You don't recognize me, I take it? No, but I suppose it was too dark to see me last night. I'm the man who held the prize money at your request."

As Hannibal jumped, the stranger drew out a thick white envelope.

"I don't like what you did to Quayle and I wouldn't mind stringing you up, myself," the white man said bluntly, "but you kept the rules of the contest and Quayle ought to have looked out for himself. You did win the money and there it is."

But he wouldn't give it to Hannibal directly, let alone shake hands or wish him luck. He put the envelope on the rickety night table.

"There! I've done what I came for."

He left without another word.

Hannibal leaped for the thick envelope as soon as the door was closed and Cindy had locked it from the inside. Cindy wasn't more excited or pleased than she had been, before. She glanced out the window and nodded this time.

"There's the wagon," she said. "Almost time to be leaving. I always knew I couldn't keep on with Felix forever, but the change is scary."

Hannibal was undoing the sealed envelope. "Now I can pay for the ride into another town, and a few more things we'll need. It makes a whole lot of difference to a man, knowing he can pay for—"

Hannibal stopped. Instead of bills, a number of sheets with writing on them had tumbled out of the envelope.

"That white bastard changed the envelopes," Hannibal began.

"Not him, or why would he come here to give it to you?"

"Then who stuffed this into the envelope?"

"Porky made the switch when he pretended he had dropped it and then picked it up," she said tiredly. "I've

124

seen him do it a dozen times before when somebody insisted that the prize money had to be held by a third party."

"Damn him," Hannibal said softly. "Damn the whole rotten bunch of 'em."

The landlady knocked on the door. Cindy shouted, "Mrs. Meek, send the man up to carry my things into the wagon. We're leaving now."

Hannibal murmured tiredly, "We are, but not for the same place, dammit."

"Don't be a fool," Cindy said sharply, scooping up the worthless papers and looking for the wastebasket. "Things are the same now as they were before. You'll pay me every cent 'cause I'll surely insist on it. The only catch is that you can't pay me yet. So don't you worry about it."

"I won't go unless I can pay my share—is anything wrong, Cindy? Don't you feel good?"

She had suddenly gasped. She had been bending over, but when she straightened she was excited.

"Look here, Hannibal." She was waving one of the worthless papers over her head as if she had just won a fight. "You can't read, I suppose."

"That's right, I can't."

"Well, I can read because Porky taught me," she said. "I had to pay for the lessons in a way that Felix never knew about, but it was the best thing I ever bought. This here is from a newspaper. Let me tell you what it says."

"No matter what it says, that can't change nothing."

"You're wrong, Han. What it says on this side of the piece of paper can change your whole life and maybe mine, too. In fact, I think it will."

There was a knock on the door and the wagon man came in. His skin was lighter than Hannibal's, as nearly everyone's was, but not much lighter. He groaned under the weight of the packing box and looked as if he couldn't possibly make it to the wagon alive with such a burden.

Hannibal finally said he'd bring down the spare boxes. The wagon man left with his burden.

"So at least you're coming out to the wagon," Cindy said quietly while the wagon man struggled in earshot.

"I wanted to get him out, so I said I'd do it."

The wagon man struggled on the stairs with his burden. Hannibal and Cindy could hear him cursing.

She spoke quietly. "The story in this paper means that the place to go is a town called Starburst. The reason is that the Governor of Alabama claims it's the town where most of the underground railroad activity in Alabama goes on. That is, smuggling coloreds up to the North, where they can be free."

"Underground railroad? Is that what you're so excited about? They're just a pack of white swindlers looking for strong colored boys to come along and sell them to new masters." He wouldn't forget his troubles with Sam Rinders for as long as he lived.

Cindy said patiently, "They aren't all like that, Hannibal, and there's no other way to get you up North without money. I'll give you a lift to Starburst and you pay me back when you get free. We can keep in touch."

"Cindy, I don't want to mess with more people like that one I met."

"You don't like 'em, and I feel pretty sure that the underground railroad whites aren't gonna be crazy 'bout you, either," Cindy said. "But the way things are now, you're all stuck with each other. Come on, Hannibal."

He thought it over, his head down to one side. When he stood, he did it slowly and carefully.

"I'll take the things down to the wagon for you," he said, and picked up a few more packages which the wagon man hadn't been able to carry.

"But you won't go?"

"I can't."

"Then I guess I'll have to play my ace," she said sadly.

126

"Mrs. Meek told me something when I left the room to ask her to send for the wagon. She told me that there's a price on your head now, Hannibal. You're wanted for murder."

Hannibal's knees buckled.

"But there were no rules to the fight and I'd have been killed if I had let Quayle go ahead and whip me. He'd have whipped me to death."

"Do you expect justice in Alabama?" she asked softly. "I knew you'd get powerful upset, Hannibal. That's why I didn't want to tell you about it unless I had to."

Hannibal nodded rigidly. "I'll go with you," he said.

She looked him up and down before leaving the room, then nodded. "Well, this has been my idea of getting a traveling friend the hard way."

CHAPTER 13

Dudley Stark swore that he wasn't going to understand women if he lived to be a hundred. Especially young women. An older one was hell on wheels, admitted, but a younger one was hell on wheels for no reason whatever and you couldn't guess what she'd say or do. Older women had certain sicknesses and they were scared of getting older, but younger ones didn't make any sense whatever.

Here he had managed to get his daughter on to a Grand Tour of Europe, scheduled to leave in just two weeks. It stood to reason that she'd be tickled to go. After all, she had been wanting it for a long time and she had been bored at Safe Harbor.

As if that hadn't been enough work for one day, he'd been forced to hire a new overseer. The one he'd had till recently, Joe Everdine, had died of a sudden heart attack. Dudley had seen to a good funeral, had spoken a few words over the grave, comforted the wife and the kids, and gone away talking with other men his age. At the funeral of a younger man there was a special terror because the same thing, could happen to somebody else today or tomorrow; and a special shame because at least he had lived longer than the other person and was glad about that.

On top of everything else, he had been trying to keep on the hunt for that infernal slave. He was going to find

Hannibal and hang the black sex fiend in his daughter's presence. What was more, he'd do it in two weeks. But there was no sign of Hannibal, look as hard as he might. In fact, Ramsey, the owner who had shanghaied Hannibal, kept saying that Hannibal had to be dead by this time.

At any rate, it had been a hellishly hard day, but a successful one by and large. Dudley had come in to supper with a feeling of self-importance that he thought to himself was pretty well justified. At least he was going to be given honor by his family as a man who got things done. Leola would probably throw her arms around him in a wild but touching burst of gratitude.

But was that the way it had happened? Of course it wasn't.

His lovely blonde daughter had no sooner heard the news than she burst into a storm of tears. Nettie, his wife, comforted her and gave him mean little looks. No wonder Dudley had stomped out of the dining room.

He was on his way to the kitchen for a few leftovers, a newspaper under his arm, when Nettie stopped him. She had helped Leola get to bed and now she was in a thoughtful mood.

"The child is convinced that we're trying to get rid of her after her recent troubles," Nettie said. "In a way, of course, she's quite right."

Dudley was stung. "You weren't exactly sympathetic to her before this, my dear."

"I'm still not sympathetic," Nettie said carefully, patting a cluster of straying gray hair back into place. "But she is terribly upset for many reasons and not too stable at the moment. I believe that her encounter with the Negro was her first experience of a sexual nature."

"It was no encounter," Dudley said fiercely. "That nigger stud forced himself on our Leola."

129

"I wish you were right," Nettie murmured.

"If there's nothing else," he said, "then I think I'll catch up with my dinner."

"There is something else, though. I came to tell you that a rider has been sent over from Mr. Ramsey."

"Is he white or black? White? Then send him into the kitchen. We can talk while I eat."

The kitchen was a huge room. In the nearest corner was a plain wooden table with two chairs. The man who entered and looked around, then nodded and came over to where Dudley had settled himself, was in his early twenties, blond, thick eyebrows. Road dust had caked on his clothes. He was trying to catch his breath.

"You work for Ramsey, do you?"

"I'm Mr. Ramsey's nephew, and he asked me to come over and tell you about a slave of yours, a black named Hannibal."

"Why, Ramsey keeps saying that Hannibal is dead or that he couldn't have survived after the whipping he took."

"My uncle admits he was wrong, sir," the young man said. When he smiled he showed a complete set of wooden false teeth. "There's been so much news about him that my uncle thinks it's unlikely you'll reach the slave fast enough to be the first to hang him."

Dudley was bursting with curiosity, but the habits of a lifetime made him remember his hospitality. "Sit down and have yourself some grub, lad."

"No, thank you, sir, not after the ride."

"Drink, then?"

"Afterwards, sir, perhaps."

The young man didn't seem inclined to talk unless he was asked a question beforehand. Dudley swore under his breath.

"What has your uncle heard about my runaway slave?"

"The slave was in a fight in the town of Brayton," the

130

youngster said. "He fought with a white man, a boxer who would go from town to town."

Nibbling at fried chicken, Dudley allowed himself to feel disappointment. The white boxer had already pulverized the slave, of course, and there was probably no room on the slave's body to inflict a fresh wound. The only thing that Dudley would be able to do would be to kill him."

"Is the slave under arrest?"

"No, Mr. Stark."

Dudley sighed regretfully. "The boxer killed him, I suppose."

"No, Mr. Stark, the slave killed the boxer. He strangled him with the ring rope and then got away."

Dudley sat back, feeling vindicated. He had been saying that the slave was dangerous, and clear proof had been given all over again. Not only had Hannibal forced himself on Dudley Stark's only child, but now he had killed a white man. His life wouldn't be safe any longer, if it had been safe for the last weeks, and whoever got to him first would probably hang him. Dudley wanted to get there first.

"How do you know beyond any doubt that it was Hannibal who did the murder?"

"The description fits, and at the end of the fight his life was saved by a nigger gal with a gun. She got him out of trouble and she called out his name. There aren't likely to be two slaves with the same name and description."

"Not likely, no." Dudley was finished with the fried chicken, and he pushed the bones to one side and out of the visitor's sight, he hoped. "Sure you won't have a drink with me? A small julep never hurt anybody over the age of consent."

The young man agreed. Dudley's mind was churning furiously as he called for a house slave to get the drinks.

131

He picked up the newspaper, still unread, and dropped it into his lap.

"It take it that Hannibal isn't in Brayton any longer, or anywhere near."

"Not as far as the town constable knows, sir," the young man said. "The nigger gal left next morning, and there was a man with her."

"And all this took place when?"

"Night before last, Mr. Stark."

The kitchen smells weren't pleasant to him any longer. He invited the young man to take his drink with him and follow into the study. Once he and his guest were in the comfortable book-lined room, Dudley began pacing.

"If Hannibal was in Brayton a couple of days ago, then he might be almost anywhere now. He could very well be out of the state and headed North."

"I suppose it's possible, sir," the young man agreed, and stood up. "I guess I'll start back now, sir. It isn't safe to be alone in the outdoors after dark."

Dudley didn't hear him or know he was gone until some moments had passed and it was too late to suggest the young man's staying overnight in one of the guest rooms. He kept on pacing more furiously than ever.

From the hallway, Nettie called, "Are you all right, dear?"

"Fine. Why shouldn't I be?"

"The way you were stomping around, it seemed to me that your guest might be uncomfortable."

Dudley's mind was churning so much that he didn't try to tell Nettie that the boy had gone a long time ago. He simply sat down on a chair, determined to give Nettie no more cause to disturb him.

He sat down on his favorite chair, put his legs on the red silk ottoman and in a moment he had kicked away the ottoman and was hitting his thighs with both hands. The thighs began to hurt, so he reached for the news-

132

paper and slapped his thighs with that; the activity didn't
help him think at all. He glared at the paper and opened
it so fiercely he tore half of one page. Glancing at it to
see if he had torn any news story that might interest him,
he suddenly caught himself looking intently at the newspaper. His back had become stiff and his eyes were alert.

The news story concerned a statement that had been
given by the Governor of the State of Alabama. The
most important part of it was simply stated that the center of abolitionist activity in Alabama was now the little
town named Starburst. Although slaves couldn't read,
they all knew the gossip that the town of Starburst was
the first station on the so-called underground railroad
smuggling slaves up North.

Dudley was out of his chair in moments. He left his
study and hurried to the door of Nettie's room. He and
his wife hadn't slept together since the early years of their
marriage, but each was welcome in the other's room.

"Well, dear," she asked, "what can I do for you?"

"Do? Do?" His wits seemed scattered to the four
winds. "Nothing at all, my dear. I came to tell you that
I'm going over to Starburst, and that I'll be there for a
few days at least."

She looked concerned. "With a new overseer on the
property, dear, don't you think that you ought to—"

"Yes, I do think so, but that damn nigger is more likely
to show up at Starburst than anywhere else, and I want to
hang him. The whole state does, come to think of it, but
I want to twist that rope in his neck myself. I'm sure you
don't blame me."

Nettie remarked mildly, "I hope our guest doesn't
hear you raising your voice, dear."

"Guest? Ramsey's nephew? The rider? He went home
a while ago. Good night, dear."

But Nettie's eyes had suddenly widened with anger
and she didn't want to let him go. "Dudley Stark, do you

133

mean to tell me that you could entertain David Ramsey's nephew in the house, a young man of your daughter's age, and not introduce him to your own daughter?"

"Introduce him? Whatever for?" Dudley's eyes bulged. "A young man comes to give me some important information and you want me to consider him as a marriage prospect? Next thing you'll want me to introduce her to newspaper sellers and bootblacks and provision merchants."

"Mr. Ramsey's nephew is hardly a provision merchant."

Dudley knew that there would be more discussion about his forgetfulness when he got back home. He made up his mind to take as long a time as was possible and sensible before getting back home. He didn't plan to come back without the slave ready to be hanged or already strung up by the neck.

As Dudley left the big house he was thinking that the trouble with women was simply that they could get obsessed over one thing and you couldn't budge them. What you had to say about men was that they were much more cool, much more temperate. A man didn't go off half-cocked about something he wanted whether it made sense or not.

Still feeling pride in himself and in the privilege of being a man, Dudley Stark mounted his best wagon and headed for Starburst in the hopeful pursuit of a slave he didn't expect he would ever see again.

CHAPTER 14

Cindy had been steered to the only boarding house in Starburst that would take colored folks. The landlady, a Mrs. Bush, agreed to give Cindy a room for several days, but sniffed disapprovingly at sight of Hannibal.

"If you want a room, you can have it separate," Mrs. Bush said.

"My friend will be staying someplace else and visiting me," Cindy said.

"Make sure his visits don't last all night," Mrs. Bush said. "I run a respectable house here and a quiet one."

Cindy nodded and smiled at Hannibal. She had understood what the landlady meant by using the word "quiet."

Cindy approved of the room. The landlady left her with Hannibal, who was looking forward to some lovemaking after the dusty ride. He put his arms around her.

"Take the hands off, Hannibal," she said, "and let me get busy."

"Get busy with me." Hannibal did take one hand away from her back, but rubbed her right breast through the dress instead.

"Hannibal, we have to find you a contact. It's important and you know it as good as I do."

He stepped back from her at last. "Let's go, then."

"It'll be a lot better if I go out alone. Nobody will con-

nect the two of us and the less you're seen around Starburst, the better."

"But what'll I do in this place by myself?"

"Count your toes if you have to." She smiled. "When
I come back, I promise we'll live it up real good. . . .
Hannibal!"

She was feeling stirred when he left and he was upset,
as well. He had stripped himself and was on the bed when
Cindy got back, but her eyes were focused on his face.

"Hannibal, it's not gonna be easy," she said. "Keep
the blanket over you like that and don't take my mind
off things. This is serious."

He sat up in bed, but he wasn't thinking about getting
her excited.

"What's wrong?"

"The white smugglers I talked to—well, they don't
want to help a slave who killed a white man."

"Why did you tell them?"

"There are reward posters out for you, Hannibal, and
you're a hard man not to describe real good. The first
smuggler who clapped eyes on you would have known."

Hannibal asked slowly, "But didn't you say that it
happened in a fight where anything goes? Didn't you
say that Felix Quayle was getting set to kill me?"

"Nothing I can say is so important as that you're a
black who killed a white man."

Hannibal said, "I knew this wouldn't work. I'll have
to run for it myself instead of hiding behind a gal's skirts.
I never should've let you talk me into doing it this way."

"You haven't been hiding behind nothing," Cindy
said, tossing her head angrily.

"Well, at least come over to me and we can be together
awhile," Hannibal said, reaching out his arms toward her.

"Not yet," she smiled, staying out of his reach.
"There's one other smuggler I have to talk to. He won't
be home until it's dark, later on."

Hannibal suggested carefully, "Maybe I should go

136

with you, Cindy. Who knows what could happen to a gal on the streets at night in a town?"

"I'll be all right. You try and get some sleep now because when I come back you'll need all the strength you can get."

He grinned. "Is that a promise, gal?"

"Sure it is."

He climbed out of bed. Cindy turned, but he reached her before she could get to the door and forced her around. His lips met hers and she responded warmly to him. He guided her hand, but she pulled it back and drew away from him.

"I'll remember that you're waiting," she said softly.

There was nothing for Hannibal to do when she left. He lay down on the bed, having made up his mind to wait for her no matter how much time it took, and he fell asleep.

It was the sound of her key in the lock that woke him. He had turned on the kerosene lamp by the time she was in the room and had locked the door again. She drew up a finger to her lips as a way of telling him to talk quietly.

"It'll be all right, Hannibal," she said, smiling broadly. "I've got hold of a man who'll do it for you."

"Are you sure he's all right?"

"Certain of it. I've talked to others of ours, who know he's done it for runaways. He isn't selling runaways back to other whites, like that fellow you told me about who tried to do that to you."

Hannibal nodded. He felt grateful and relieved, but he hoped there wouldn't be any more talk about it for a while.

"Well," he said, getting out of bed and close to Cindy, "what are we waiting for? The bed's warm and I'm sizzling, gal, believe me."

"Nothing's gonna happen between us tonight, Hannibal," she said firmly. "Tonight is when you leave."

"Not so soon!"

137

"And the sooner the better, Hannibal. Every second might count."

But Hannibal reached for his woman, clothes and all, and forced her down on the big wide comfortable bed. Cindy protested, but Hannibal took off her clothes swiftly and touched her in secret places. Time disappeared as Hannibal and Cindy brought each other to one roaring and gasping climax and then to another. Time was nowhere in sight, nowhere in consciousness.

Arthur Davis stayed in his general store till eleven o'clock on certain nights only. He would generally sit in the back room on those nights, hands folded, eyes half-shut. When somebody passed on the wooden boards in front of this row of stores his eyes would open wide as he waited for the signal ring that the door was being opened. Generally, though, his late-night patrons, as he sometimes thought of them in a joking way, would come in by the back entrance. He kept the front locked, as a rule, late at night.

Some nights he would find himself making sales in the store. Mrs. Lasker, over at the northeast end of town, generally waited for her supplies until he would be open late. When he spent a whole month without late hours one time, he supposed she must have been pretty badly inconvenienced. One night she had bought ten dollars worth .of provisions, which was more money than he had taken in for the entire day.

Keeping open late was in many ways a bother to him after a hard day's work. It would raise merry hell with Evelyn, for instance, who hated for him to do it. Even the kids would start to whine and slobber. Tonight, as it happened, Evelyn had been nearly in tears.

"Not another one of *those?*" she had asked.

"I can't help it."

Evelyn had sniffed. She was a Clark from near Bir-

138

mingham, with the family's pale complexion, and tears gave her a splotchy face. The kids were the same way, and at his and Evelyn's wedding, Arthur's mother-in-law-to-be had looked like her face was covered with acid stains.

"What'll we do if you get arrested?" Evelyn asked helplessly.

"I've never had the slightest troubles, Evelyn, and you know it."

"But what if it does happen? Suppose Sheriff Perkins comes here one night and brings up on charges of smuggling you-know-what, Arthur?"

"If he does, I'll say I'm innocent. If he has any proof, he'll have to haul it out. But there can't be any proof and you know it."

"If he takes you to jail and you have to be there until you can be tried, the store will be lost to us. I can't handle it and I'll have to sell."

"Look here, Evelyn, if there's even the slightest chance of my getting in trouble, I'll quit doing the extra work. I promise you that. I'm nobody's fool."

"But you won't know you're in trouble until it's too late." She sniffed. "It isn't as if you made so much money at doing that thing."

"Every little extra helps, woman. But as I tell you, if there's the slightest whisper of trouble I'll give it up permanently."

Not until he was at the door of their cabin, though, did she make the strongest single argument.

"It's not as if you were taking chances on your freedom on account of principle," Evelyn said. "It's not as if you liked Negroes or felt particularly sorry for them."

It was true, of course. Arthur Davis sat in the store and waited for another runaway slave to come in and told himself how true it was. He had made arrangements

139

with the slave's gal, and he guessed from her hesitation that the slave had done some crime or other. Arthur Davis wasn't like most of the underground railroad people in Starburst; he didn't care what a runaway had done, only that he'd get paid for the smuggling when he dropped the slave off.

Footsteps sounded on wooden boards, but it was somebody in shoes. Slaves generally went barefoot, even if they were such fools as to try and come here by the front door. Arthur relaxed.

It wasn't actually true that he didn't like coloreds. He didn't have any feelings about them one way or the other. Every so often an abolitionist type would say that every white man ought to feel guilty about what was happening in the country, even though he personally may not have had a big part in it. But if the white man felt guilty enough he would be spending his time leading raids on plantations and freeing slaves; he wouldn't be talking about it.

Sometimes a Negro speaker at the Town Hall, a free man, would point to a whole audience of people without slave property and he would say:

"*You* are keeping *me* in slavery."

Not only wouldn't anybody in the audience ever laugh, but no one ever jumped up and called the speaker a liar. People listened and were polite to a Negro speaker and wouldn't let him close to their own private thoughts.

Sometimes, though, there would be a convincing speaker, nearly always white, at Town Hall or in church. Arthur, like everybody else, would leave the scene of that speech feeling that all Negroes had been misunderstood and weren't appreciated and had been handled unfairly and that no white man could do enough to make up for what had happened to the Negroes in this country. But then he would go out to the street and run into some example of arrogance and boorishness from a free

140

colored man or woman or even a child. As a result his feelings would get all mixed up, and he figured that nobody could understand why Negroes were treated the way they were until he knew some of them.

It was near eleven o'clock and the runaway hadn't made his appearance. Arthur had said he wouldn't wait longer than that, and he didn't. He made ready to close the store until morning, leaving a kerosene lantern light in the back room so it would seem that somebody was still in the place. He was always hearing about robberies of store owners and he never did know what precautions a man might take that he hadn't taken as yet. He left a box of postage stamps on the counter at closing and always left some coins in the cash box; otherwise, if robbers came in they might do some damage out of anger.

Just as he was closing the back door and walking around to the front, he saw two dim figures move in the street. He could see them by the glass of the front door. He tested the door to make certain it was locked and then turned around casually.

The figures had been walking on the row of wooden boards that faced him, but they must have hidden themselves in storefronts when they saw him.

Calmly he called out, "Who is that?"

No response. He was sure that if he had been in any danger he would have been attacked before shutting the store.

He took something of a chance and called, "Is that you, boy? Your gal with you?"

A white man's voice suddenly said impatiently, "I had a sure tip you were the contact and it was right."

A man walked out of a store front opposite Arthur, then stepped down into the mud. He jumped onto the boards and took two steps until he was facing Arthur. He was a big man with a mustache and a red face. By the glow of gas lamps on each corner, he looked as if he was angry. Arthur waited, fists in his pockets, ready to defend himself if he had to.

"Getting all set to smuggle some runaway out of town, huh? And I know who the runaway was. A big black named Hannibal. A murdering raping bastard of a nig—"

Arthur had found his courage at last. "I don't know what you're talking about."

"No? You keep the store open for three extra hours with not a customer in the place."

"I had to do some work."

"Sure, and we saw you at it, too, sitting in the chair like you were half-dead. You hardly moved from that chair for the whole three hours."

Arthur wasn't so upset about being caught in a lie as at the use of the word "we." He looked around in the darkness, but saw nobody.

"I don't know what you're talking about, but this is your word against mine and nobody else's. Get out of my way or you'll be sorry."

The newcomer said softly, "Take one step away from me and you're a dead man."

Arthur believed him.

A familiar voice he hadn't heard all evening called out, "I think this has gone far enough."

Arthur couldn't help looking away and toward the other set of boards. Constable Isaiah Perkins was coming towards them. Perkins was a heavy man, and everybody in town hated the idea of having a fat constable, but people voted for him time after time.

Perkins approached the two men. "I thought I'd stop a murder, if that's at all possible."

Almost as soon as he spoke, they heard a shout from a few blocks down. It was followed by the unmistakable sound of fists on flesh. Perkins, listening with his head down, suddenly straightened and shrugged. He was at ease again.

"Some nigger work over there," he said. "I can tell from the voice. I'll probably hear about it in the morning."

The man who had been with the constable, and whose name Arthur didn't know was Dudley Stark, looked irritated. "Suppose one of them gets killed?"

"In that case we'll bury him and have us one nigger less." Perkins smiled. "One reason we get so much smuggling of niggers in this town is that we don't like niggers, whether they're free or not. Right, Arthur?"

"If you say so, sheriff."

Dudley Stark frowned. He had never thought of liking or hating somebody because that person was colored. He hated a slave called Hannibal, but for personal reasons.

"All I'm concerned about is one nigger called Hannibal," Dudley Stark pointed out. "I want him and I'm willing to save the State of Alabama the expense of feeding him and putting him on trial for murder. He's my property and I mean to hang him."

Perkins said, "You haven't heard any disagreement from me, Mr. Stark."

Dudley Stark turned to Arthur. "Now the rumor in Starburst is that you're the man most likely to smuggle out a slave without caring if he is wanted for any crime or not. I warn you that if I find you helping Hannibal, I'm going to wring your neck before you get put into prison."

The threat of violence didn't worry Arthur nearly as much as that of being put in prison. He turned away from Stark and the sheriff, walking toward the wagon which would take him home. When he got there, he would let his wife know that he was finished with the slave-smuggling business. Evelyn would be so set up about his decision that she would probably let him have what he wanted but hadn't had for a long time.

As it happened, as soon as he put the decision into ef-

143

fect and turned down a chance to smuggle a pair of slaves out of Alabama a few nights later, he became known to his friends as a man who talked in favor of abolishing slavery. He made any number of heartrending speeches on the subject and could always be counted on for a contribution to any charity to help colored people.

CHAPTER 15

It never would have happened if Hannibal hadn't left Cindy later than he expected. They had been making love and enjoying each other's bodies for an hour or so. Cindy would think of something to do that she had never done with him before and she would do it, giving Hannibal more pleasure than ever. Hannibal would touch her in this place or that place and she would gasp like a train going into a tunnel.

But he did have to go away, and when the time came for him to do it he was later than he could have guessed. The streets were dark. Cindy went with him to show him where to go. They had made plans for him to write to a friend of hers when he was safe. The address had been written down by Cindy and Hannibal had put it in a pocket.

It was late and Hannibal didn't expect trouble, or maybe he was dreaming at the idea of being free and in the north. He didn't hear footsteps behind him; and when he tried to defend himself it was too late. One man had put an arm around his neck and somebody else punched him on the body at first and then on the head with something hard. Just before everything turned dark, Hannibal realized that the men who were doing this to him were a pair of niggers. Then he wasn't conscious . . .

"Where's the gal?" the wiry one asked.

"She ran like a bat outta hell."

"I thought I'd get some chances with her."

"You might get some chances in the nigger jail if we don't hurry," the heavy one said.

"Let's take him and see if he's got money. At least we ought to get us something for tonight if not a gal."

They dumped Hannibal into a wagon, which they drove to a quiet section outside the limits of Starburst. When one of the men got off the wagon, he patted the horse.

"Nice-lookin' nag. Maybe we can keep this outfit. Best we ever stole, if y'ask me."

"If we keep this we can't go back into Starburst."

"The hell with Starburst, then."

The wiry man had finished searching Hannibal and had drawn out some papers with writing and printing on them.

"Money?" the heavy one asked.

"Just this stuff. Are these anything, you suppose?"

"They're freedom papers," the heavy one said. "Poor bastard! Just been set free and don't know what to do."

"He had that gal with him, so he knew what to do." The wiry one raised the papers high. "Can we get money for these?"

"Probably, from a smuggler. He could give a slave these papers in case any questions should get asked, and then the papers are mailed back to Starburst."

"We'll take 'em, then." And Hannibal's falsified freedom papers were stuffed into a slim pocket. "There ain't another nickel to be got out of him unless—"

"We have to dump him, that's all."

"Unless we sell him," the wiry one said. "A slave without his freedom papers is still a slave. This one is big and strong, so we could get some money for him."

"Almost a shame to do it to one of ours," the heavy one murmured.

"He'd probably do the same thing to both of us, but we just happened to be first."

The heavy one sighed. "Who needed him? All we

wanted was a chance to grab the gal with him and have ourselves a good time with her."

"Let's make the best of what we've got," the wiry man said.

"Okay. Where'll we start?"

"Oxnard, I guess. We get more money out of there when we have a deal going than any other place."

"That's a good idea."

"Well, I don't get any other kind."

Oxnard was a plantation in easy traveling distance of Starburst. The two men, moving quickly, reached the grounds and made for the small house that the overseer had been allowed to use. The wiry one knocked boldly on the door while the heavy one looked around, worried. The door was opened by a chunky Negro with hard eyes and strong hands.

"What do you two want?"

"Want to do you a favor."

On the bed against the far wall, a Negro girl stirred in restless sleep. She called out, "Please don't ask me to do that again, Willy. Not again."

"Well?" the Negro overseer asked roughly. "Make it quick and get out."

"We've got a big buck in the wagon and there are no papers on him," the wiry one said, keeping himself from looking over at the bed. His heavy friend, though, couldn't take eyes away from the gal.

The overseer asked, "You trying to sell him?"

"Right as rain."

In her sleep the gal pleaded, "I'll do anything else you want! Anything! But don't ask me to do that, please don't!"

The overseer said quickly, "I never take boys from nowhere. You two ought to know better than that. Now get outta here and let me try for some sleep."

"Any suggestions where we can take him?"

"Try Joe Cleeve. He might be okay."

147

The wiry man had to tap the heavy one to remind him that they were leaving. As the heavy man stumbled back to the darkness he and his friend heard the girl's sudden wide-awake shouts.

"Don't hit me there, oh please? I'll do what you want, I'll do everything, but don't hit me *there!* I'll do—"

The heavy man, walking away as if he was in a trance, licked his lips.

"I wonder what he gets that gal to do," he said hoarsely.

"So do I," the wiry one admitted, "and if we get enough money outta this buck we can try it with different gals till we find out. Willy woulda bought this buck if not for wanting to slip it to that gal."

Hannibal was still unconscious in the back of the wagon. The heavy man climbed up on the buckboard next to the wiry one. He was sighing.

"We going to try Joe Cleeve next?" the heavy one asked.

"Unless you got a better idea."

He didn't wait to find out, but started the wagon on the move. The heavy one shivered in the hot night, but didn't make any remark.

The wire man pulled the wagon to a stop in front of an overseer's shack. From the whipping post, which was further away than either man guessed, they could hear a muffled moaning. The moon, hanging above them like something on wires, looked as if it would be greasy to the touch.

The white man who opened the door to them was thin-lipped and small-eyed. He looked both Negroes up and down, then sighed.

"We'll talk out there," he said, rather than inviting them to his cabin. He closed his door and led the way to a grove of trees. As soon as he reached the clearing, he whirled around to them.

"Well? Why are you coming around so late at night?"

"We've got a buck for you. Good worker."

148

Joe Cleeve pursed his lips, then sighed and shook his head. "Wish I could take him."

"You've always taken the others."

"My boss has passed the word down: no slaves without papers that give us a clear title."

The wiry one said mildly, "I didn't think he was so crazy about the letter of the law."

"He isn't." Joe Cleeve had the nastiest smile of any white man that either of the blacks had ever seen. "Just that those others try harder to get away, and that causes us some more trouble than we need."

"I can see as it would."

Joe Cleeve grinned wolfishly. "There are some of our niggers who think we don't treat 'em right."

The heavy one shuddered. The wiry one closed his eyes briefly.

Joe Cleeve drew his head back and laughed. "All I can say to you boys is that you should always carry papers on you to show you're free."

"We do," the wiry one said flatly. "Now have you got any idea what we could do with this buck we've got?"

"I'm not an employment bureau," Joe Cleeve sneered, and made a motion with the hands as if to send the two men away. The heavy man actually turned to go back to the wagon, but the wiry one faced Cleeve. "What are you waiting for?"

"We've done you so many favors that we're entitled to one in return," the wiry man said, talking determinedly over a fresh gust of groaning from the direction of the whipping post. "If you've got any idea where we can get rid of this one, we want you to tell us."

"I haven't got the slightest notion," Joe Cleeve began. As the wiry one finally turned, exasperated, he was surprised at first to hear Joe Cleeve ask, "What's in it for me?"

The wiry one said promptly, "If we get a hundred for him, we'll give you ten."

"Twenty."

The wiry man sighed. "You'd probably steal the flowers off your mother's grave."

"Let's not talk about ethics," Cleeve said thinly. "Either you want to do business or you don't."

"Do," the wiry man said.

"Harry Fazenda has got a new job for himself," Cleeve said, "and I'm pretty sure he wants to make a good record at the start. He wouldn't mind picking up somebody, I don't think, and he's the only one I can figure right now."

"Where is Harry Fazenda at?"

"He's the new foreman at—" Joe Cleeve snapped his fingers, irritated. "Damn it, the place has got a funny name and I can never remem—oh yes, I can. Safe Harbor. The owner is named Dudley Stark." Cleeve smiled. "I'll tell you exactly how to get there."

The wagon ride took longer than either man expected, and it was dawn of an oven-warm day before the two men found themselves on the grounds at Safe Harbor.

To one of the slaves the wiry man said, "Tell your overseer to come out to meet us, and tell him it's important."

The slave nodded, frightened, and ran. When he came back, some moments later, he wasn't nearly as frightened; but there wasn't anybody with him, either.

"Mister Harry says to come with me," the slave said.

The two men nodded. The heavy one glanced back to the wagon. The buck's position had changed, probably on account of the bumpy ride; but he was breathing every bit as evenly as before, his body was relaxed, and his eyes were shut lightly.

The two men were led to a long cabin at the base of the fields. A scowling white man, his face reddened from the Alabama sun, glanced at them as they came in and then looked outside to where the slaves worked. He

150

didn't look at the visitors too often during the conversation.

"Lazy buggers," he murmured at one point. "I told 'em I'd keep an eye on who was working and who wasn't. Now I can prove to 'em that I really mean what I say."

"Mister Harry?" the wiry one started. "Mister Joe Cleeve sent us over."

"If I wasn't so good-natured I'd let that Rufus have it with the rope-end of a whip," the overseer said, still looking outside. "Just because he's fat and the gals don't give him any never-mind, he thinks he can do anything he wants. I'll have to learn him different."

"Mister Harry," the wiry one said patiently, "if you listen to us and we can go that much faster, then you'll feel a whole lot better and so will we."

"Go on, boys. I may not look, but I'm listening."

"We've got a strong buck in our wagon and we're offering him out cheap."

"Papers?"

"No papers at all."

Harry Fazenda turned to the men. "Where'd you get him?"

"If you really want to know," the wiry one said blandly, "I'll only have to work harder at figuring out a good story."

Fazenda stared at him. "I guess you wouldn't have the least bit of trouble doing that."

"You're right."

"If this buck is strong, I'll admit we could sure use somebody like him around here. I don't think there's a good worker in a wagonload."

"This one is so strong he's gotta be good."

"With no papers, though, I don't see how I can use him."

"Now, Mister Harry, I'm sure you know good like I do just the way these things get done," the wiry one said.

151

"You're dead certain to have papers of some runaways and you can show them in case there should be any questions. Your boss will think he's got a good overseer because this buck will cost you a lot less than he would cost at a slave auction."

"I suppose that's true," Harry Fazenda admitted. "I shouldn't say it, but there are papers for one big buck who ran out and who Mister Stark is anxious to get hold of. I could probably switch those papers around, I suppose."

"Then we're in business," the wiry man said. Now that he thought of it, he hadn't eaten since early last night and he was damnably hungry.

"If he's as big and as strong as you say, I can offer you some money for him," Fazenda said.

Something in the man's offhand tone made the wiry one ask, "How much is 'some'?"

"Fifty dollars is the best I can do."

"For fifty dollars, Mister Harry, you can have a choice of one arm or leg," the wiry man said. "I think you ought to take the arm because it can do more work. How much work it can do without the rest of the body I don't know, but for fifty dollars you'll be able to find out."

"Is this a joke?" Fazenda asked, startled.

"Pretty much, yes," the wiry man admitted. "He'll cost you two hundred dollars."

"If he's as big as you say I'll go up to seventy-five," Fazenda said. "Not a penny more."

"All right, you've come up so I'll go down. I'm willing to take a hundred and fifty."

"Sure you are. But will you take seventy-five?"

"At least make it a hundred. We don't have to jaw around like this for hours and you know it's a fair price."

Fazenda nodded finally. "Good enough. Now let's take a look at him."

As they left the cabin Fazenda shouted, "Keep busy up

there! I want that whole row cleared by the time I get back or there'll be trouble."

He turned away, blinked, then turned back. "Where in hell is that fat nigger, Rufus? He was just there a little while ago. Where'd he get to?"

If not for the two slave dealers at his side, he would probably have asked some nasty questions of the Negroes who were hard at their back-breaking work. As it was, he turned and followed the wiry man toward the wagon. The heavy one, looking around hopefully for the sight of some slave girls, brought up the rear.

The stolen wagon loomed at the bottom of the field. The wiry man blinked and then asked his companion:

"Do you see what I do?"

The heavy man glanced out at the wagon. "It looks shakier, if you know what I mean."

"You left it so it was straight behind the horse, but now it's almost at the horse's left side."

The heavy man started to run toward the wagon. He glanced into the back of it, then looked up. His jaw had dropped in surprise, but he didn't know or care.

The wiry man didn't have to look into the rear of the wagon. He shut his eyes tightly as if he was in sudden agony.

"Must'a climbed up and crawled out," the heavy man said, hardly able to understand what had happened. "It couldn't be any other way."

"He can't have been out of the wagon long enough to get off the grounds," the wiry man said. "He's still on the plantation."

"I'll tell you what," Fazenda said. "You boys drop by in a week and I'll let you know if he's here. If he is, I'll pay you what I owe."

The wiry man said nothing, but climbed into the wagon. The heavy man clambered in next to him. Fazenda returned to the fields as the men started off, but they saw him give orders to one of the field slaves.

153

"When we come back, Fazenda will tell us he hasn't seen nothing and don't know nothing," the wiry man said bitterly. "Maybe he'll give us a dollar apiece for our trouble."

The heavy man, still considering what had happened before, said thoughtfully, "I only wish that whites wouldn't call us 'boy.' I don't like that."

The wiry man snapped, "You let him go, practically, so you're not only a boy but you're a nigger. There's nothing worse than that."

PART THREE

CHAPTER 16

Hannibal never knew exactly what happened. When he came to think about it, a long time afterwards, he could remember a splitting headache and he could remember bumping against wood and plopping down to a dusty road.

He couldn't walk and it was easy to crawl, so he crawled. Sun pounded him, earth punished his hands and kneecaps, thirst raged in him.

He never knew just when he lost his balance. One second he was crawling along and then he started to tumble down a wooded slope. He couldn't call out and he didn't know how to stop himself. He saw the sky as a semicircle and then the earth as a semicircle. A crooked tree was near him and he put up both hands to shield himself. Not for the first time the world became black and around him was nothing and he himself was nothing. . . .

He was on a straw pallet when his eyes opened and he was not in the open air. He didn't know where he was, but he was hoping he could get back to Cindy as soon as possible.

When his eyes cleared he saw that the room was filled with straw pallets, one of them almost next to another. There was hardly any space between. It reminded him of the slave pens at Safe Harbor.

He was frantically trying to clear his head when the door opened on the fat and shambling Rufus.

"Boy, you've really done it this time," Rufus said carefully. "How do you feel?"

"Bad." Hannibal tried to swallow. "I know this isn't a dream. Who brought me back here?"

"A pair of our people." Rufus sniffed. "Came to sell you, not knowing Master Dudley has been after you."

"I have to get out." Frantically he tried to get up, but couldn't.

"Better you rest for now," Rufus said, and sniffed. "I sure wish somebody would try and sell a pretty gal over here."

Hannibal, though his head was splitting, understood that the fat slave still wasn't able to get what he wanted from any of the slave gals at Safe Harbor.

"Could I have some water?" he asked, not able to raise his voice above a whisper.

"Certain sure." Rufus looked worried, though, when he brought the water in a cracked cup. "Mister Harry is on the way here and I can't get out. I'm s'posed to be in the fields right now and I sure am anyplace else but."

"Who is Mister Harry?"

"The new overseer."

"Didn't he know I was here?"

"Saw you start to crawl away from the wagon and went after you on my own and without a word to anybody else," Rufus said. "Dragged you back here 'cause Mister Harry would see me if I tried taking you anyplace else on the plantation. He'll see me if I leave here now, so I better stay."

The door opened on a big white man with a sunburned face. He wrinkled his nose at the slave pen smell. Then his eyes narrowed angrily.

"I'm not surprised you're here instead of working, Rufus," he said, standing with feet apart. "You're putting

156

me into a position I don't like. Sooner or later I'm going to have to glue you down across the whipping post and let you have twenty juicy ones. And it'll be your own fault."

"Yessuh." Rufus shuffled his feet in an inch of space between pallets.

"Get out and back to the fields before I do the job on you right now and with my own hands." He suddenly whirled. "Who are you?"

"Obie is very sick, Mister Harry," Rufus said. "I came back to see if I couldn't do something for him."

"Another boy wasting good time." The new overseer walked over to where Hannibal lay. He looked down at him intently. "What's been happening to you, boy? Too many watermelons?"

"Fell," Hannibal said carefully. "Fell, Mister Harry."

Nothing in Hannibal's life had ever been harder than bringing out those few words. He lay on the foul-smelling pallet and waited to be called by name and then pulled out and hanged for his crimes.

But the new overseer only said, "Yes, you've been having a bad time. I can see that. Was it a fight?"

"No, Mister Harry. I fell, like I said."

"I wouldn't think there was anybody strong enough around here to do you so much damage," the overseer agreed moodily. He turned to go and then suddenly looked back. He was rubbing his reddened cheeks thoughtfully. "I don't know as I've seen you before."

Rufus, playing for time, said, "Seen who, Mister Harry? Obie here? Why, he's been at Safe Harbor forever. His folks was house slaves and I think even the folks of his folks belonged to Master Dudley's—"

"I'd have sworn—" Harry Fazenda frowned. "I've been working hard these last few days, but not hard enough to forget a big buck like you."

He suddenly turned back. "You aren't the new boy

157

who was just brought over, by any chance? You didn't get sick on the way when you tried to get out of the wagon—or did you? Go on, tell me the truth. I won't raise any hell about that."

Rufus, sticking to his story, said, "I dunno what you could mean, Mister Harry."

"I think you're lying," Fazenda said, "but I'll check it out. If you're lying just to try and prove you can think faster than I can, boy, you're in for trouble."

"I'm telling the truth, Mister Harry."

"What's your name, boy?" he asked Hannibal.

"Obie, Mister Harry."

"Is that short for Obadiah?"

"Yes, Mister Harry."

"I'll look into this, boy," Fazenda said, and sniffed. "I can see you aren't going anywhere for a while."

He laughed shortly and then walked out of the slave pen. Rufus, looking after him through the partly opened door, could see him pause to take a deep breath and then go back toward the fields, where others were hard at work.

Hannibal raised himself slightly on the straw pallet. "What am I supposed to do? Soon as he asks around he'll find out there isn't an Obadiah and then he'll point me out to Master Dudley to show he was so smart he got hold of a new slave for no money to mention. And when Master Dudley gets one look at me, I'll be in line to get my neck stretched."

"We have to wait till Mister Harry is back in the fields or close to 'em, and then we get you away from here. If we can get it done between us, Hannibal."

"Not you," Hannibal said carefully. "Go back to the fields or you really get yourself whipped bad. No sense in that, Rufus."

"And leave you alone?"

"I'll make it."

"You didn't make it so good when you tumbled your-self outta that wagon," Rufus said sternly.

"You won't make it too good if you get hanged with me."

Rufus sighed, then turned and started to leave. At the door he looked around long enough to see that Hannibal was still lying quietly on the straw pallet.

"Hannibal, you damn fool, if you can get out of here by yourself, do it now. There ain't no such thing as a soft rope."

Hannibal waited till Rufus was out of sight before trying to stand up. He felt much better now that he had been lying down and he'd had some water to drink. His constitution had always been strong.

He sat up and realized that he had suddenly felt a wave of dizziness. Carefully he leaned forward, tried to fold his legs under him, and then got up. He couldn't make it. Dizzy and weak, he fell back against the straw pallet. He had tricked himself into this place, and now he couldn't get away without help that might cost Rufus his own life. All that was left for Hannibal, it seemed, was to be hanged.

No, he wouldn't stand for this. He wouldn't get his neck stretched like a turkey at Thanksgiving.

Again he sat up, dizzy and weak. Again he tried to put his feet under him and stand. For a moment he thought he was going to make it, but then he toppled over. He knew he was going to faint once more and that he'd be completely helpless no matter what happened.

Toward the end of the day, Rufus saw Sarah Jane in the fields. It was Sarah Jane who had thought of herself as wanting Hannibal so much that she had practically de-stroyed Hannibal's chances to escape with the gal he had really loved, with Miriam. Whenever Rufus saw Sarah Jane he sighed a little because she was so pretty.

159

When Sarah Jane saw Rufus, on the other hand, she tried as best she could to keep out of his way. Otherwise he would almost certainly make a grab for her.

Rufus started to giggle when he saw Sarah Jane, and the gal couldn't help turning towards him. They were on the way back from the fields and it was evening.

"What's riding you?" Sarah Jane asked.

"Nothing, nothing." But he kept giggling.

Sarah Jane tossed her head. "I wouldn't ask what you're riding 'cause I know it's only yourself."

The giggle vanished. "What does that mean?"

"Means I don't like to be laughed at."

But the giggle returned almost as soon as she said that. "Can't help it, Sarah Jane. If you knew what I do, then you'd be splitting your sides, too."

"You expect everybody is stupid like you and don't know nothing and can go around giggling all the time?"

"You can't make me feel bad now, Sarah Jane. It's just that I know something as would interest you a whole lot, but I won't say what it is."

Sarah Jane shrugged. There wasn't anything that might interest her and him, both. She'd been sleeping with a boy named Samson, who wasn't nearly as strong as the original Samson had been; and Rufus was probably jealous.

But Rufus had thought of himself as a friend of Hannibal's, and he had known how interested in Hannibal she had been. Rufus was looking at the male slave pens, which were now in sight, and when he turned to her again he had gone back to giggling. Her eyes followed his, and then she turned to the fat slave, this time of her own free will.

"Are you telling me that he's back?" she whispered. "Is that it?"

Rufus was alarmed. He put up both hands in front of his body as if to shield himself from a punch.

"I haven't said anything like that."

But Sarah Jane smiled this time. "Where is he, Rufus? He can't be in there 'cause he'd be sure to be found. Tell me where is Hannibal, Rufus."

"I'll tell you," he said, lowering his voice and straightening himself, "if you'll do something for me."

"What do you mean?"

"Just touch me in that place once, Sarah Jane," the fat slave pleaded. "Please touch me."

Sarah Jane made a face, not wanting to get closer to the fat slave. There didn't seem any harm in promises, though.

"I'll do better than that, Rufus honey."

"Now?"

"After supper, Rufus. I'll meet you out there."

And she gestured toward a grove of trees which many slaves used for their lovemaking. In the clearing beyond that grove, Hannibal and Miriam had made love, and Hannibal had probably made love with Sarah Jane long before he realized how much he cared for Miriam.

"Then that's when I'll tell you what you want to know," Rufus said, and turned away.

Sarah Jane said carefully, "What you tell me had better be true, Rufus honey, and I better see proof."

"You will. You will."

"Otherwise," she said carefully, "I'll cut your gizzard open."

He turned to her and smiled foolishly. If he had felt even the slightest flicker of fear, she couldn't tell from his behavior.

"Can't I—well, have something to remember you by?"

"Even for a few minutes?"

"Yes."

He had positioned himself so that the lower part of his grotesque body was extended towards her. He wanted her to squeeze him lightly between the crotch with a cupped hand.

Sarah Jane smiled, then put up two fingers to her lips

161

and kissed them and drew out the fingers in a semi-circle.

"Just a kiss, Rufus, until I see you again," she said lightly, and laughed.

The fat slave called out as if he was in pain, which in a way he was.

Sarah Jane was chuckling as she walked toward the women's slave pens. She'd see Rufus later on, of course, and she'd put him off then and try to find out what he knew about Hannibal. She certainly wouldn't let him touch her.

As for Rufus, he walked into the men's area. He wasn't absolutely sure whether or not he would see Hannibal on one of the straw pallets.

Harry Fazenda had been an overseer on two other plantations in the last half a dozen years, and had got himself a reputation as a quiet but effective worker. He didn't want to stir up trouble and in most situations he was willing to live and let live. If a slave got away with some minor piece of rule-breaking that didn't affect the work, Harry was more willing than not to give that slave a lecture and do absolutely nothing else about it. He wouldn't whip a slave himself and had only a few times given instructions to one of the other boys to do the whipping. He had never struck a slave in his life, mainly because he found the skin color repulsive and couldn't help thinking that the black or brown stuff would rub off on him somehow if he did touch one of them.

There was a room near the cellar of the main house which Dudley Stark used as an office. Fazenda went down the stairs and opened the room, not glancing down toward the cellar. He turned on the kerosene lamp, blew an inch of dust off the desk and looked for the slave records.

When he was finished, several moments later, he was confused. There had indeed been a slave named Obadiah,

162

but the *d* on the bottom of the record might mean that the slave had died. In Dudley Stark's so-called record system, though, the *d* might mean something else.

All the same, Harry Fazenda wasn't the man to keep from getting to the bottom of things. He put the records away, wondering when Dudley Stark would get back.

On his way to the main floor of the big house he encountered Miss Leola. Mr. Dudley Stark's daughter was sitting casually and looking into the distance. There was a book open in front of her, but she wasn't reading it. Nor had she bothered to straighten the straw-blonde hair that lay so close to her eyes. She was wearing a forest green dress with a leaf-shaped sprig of black lace at the throat.

"Congratulations, Miss Leola," he called out heartily. "I understand you're leaving soon for Europe."

"Yes. Yes." Leola Stark didn't seem to be very enthusiastic about the trip. "Very soon now I'll be going."

"Miss Leola, I wouldn't want to bother you," he began, as her eyes strayed from him, "but I wonder if you'd know whether we've got a slave called Obadiah."

Leola frowned, either at the interruption of her thoughts or at an effort of recollection. Fazenda was on the point of apologizing when she looked directly at him.

"I know we've had a slave of that name, but I think he died."

"Yes, I kind of suspected that." Fazenda shrugged. He told himself that Rufus had been a fool for telling lies that could be proved wrong. "Well, thanks very much, Miss Leola."

"Not at all." Leola kept on frowning, though. "What does he look like?"

"Very dark, very big," Fazenda said. "He's been sick and he keeps saying his name is Obadiah; and another slave, who started this story, is getting it backed up."

"Sick, is he? In the slave pens?"

163

"Yes, that's right. It's nothing serious, though. He'll probably be up and working tomorrow, Miss Leola. We won't have lost too much."

"We *might* have another Obadiah on the plantation for all I know," Leola said, a catch in her voice. "I'm not absolutely sure. What you'll have to do is to ask my daddy about it tomorrow or whenever he comes back from Starburst. I'm sure it'll be tomorrow—aren't you?"

"I suppose you're right, Miss Leola. Sorry to have disturbed you. I guess I'll be going to my cabin to get some rest. After a day in the fields, a man needs it."

Leola had controlled her excitement when the overseer was in the same room with her, but as soon as he left she nearly called out with pleasure. She tried to stand up quickly, but in her excitement she lost her balance and had to sit down again for a moment.

She knew that description and it only fit one slave she had ever seen, one slave she had ever known of. It was Hannibal who had come back to Bon Repos. It had to be!

And she knew why he had done it. He had come back to get her, to get Leola Stark and bring her away with him. She couldn't doubt it. Hannibal had come back, risking his life for her. It was just the sort of thing that happened in romantic stories which Leola sometimes read, and it was thrilling but not surprising.

She would go with him to the ends of the earth, of course, but first she had to find him. Not for a moment did she doubt that for her to go outside and in the general direction of the slave pens would be the best way to find her Hannibal.

She shrugged a shawl around her, in case there should be a nip in the air, and left by the back way.

Fazenda was stepping out the main entrance of the big house, pretending he owned it and all the land in sight. His step was firmer, his manner more relaxed. There was

164

even a small contemptuous smile on his thin lips for the people who had to work for the master of this house and the land around it.

The smile was wiped off when he saw Dudley Stark coming towards the entrance. Fazenda the landowner went back to being Fazenda the overseer who needed his job and wanted to make a good impression on his employer.

Dudley Stark looked drawn and tired. His clothes drooped on him.

"Didn't have any luck," he said tiredly. "The damned nigger seems to have gone. I came back home to get some sleep and make sure my family doesn't worry about me."

Fazenda took pity on him. "Well, Mr. Stark, I think I can give you some good news to balance the bad."

"I can use it, Harry." He suddenly cocked his head to one side. "Did you hear a door open and close? At the rear of the house, I'm pretty sure."

"No, Mr. Stark, I can't say that I did."

"Well, I don't suppose it makes a never-mind," Dudley Stark decided. "What's your news?"

In as few words as he could manage, Fazenda told about the slave sellers and his trying to look for the slave who had suddenly escaped.

"Sounds as slippery as this buck nigger I'm looking for these days," Dudley Stark grumbled, running a hard hand through his graying hair. "Did you find him?"

"Yes, Mr. Stark, I did." Fazenda told about the slave being sick and about Rufus inventing a story to explain his being at the slave pens in order to keep him, Fazenda, from being suspicious until the slave could get his strength back and go.

"I plan to keep him, though," Fazenda said with relish. "First thing in the morning—he can't move around much unless he's stronger than Hercules—I aim to go out to the slave pens and lay down the law to him. Here he is and here he stays unless he wants to be lynched."

"If he isn't ours we don't need him," Dudley Stark said, surprising his new overseer. "For all you know, Harry, this slave might be diseased. A colored man catches the pox as easily as the two of us manage to breathe."

"Never saw a healthier specimen than this one, Mr. Stark. Good constitution, you can see. He's as big—"

"I don't hold with press-gang slavery," Dudley Stark said. "I've seen too many men who tried it and were sorry afterwards. Your slave who's been forced into service and isn't a slave to begin with, gets sour and resentful. He starts the other slaves on a course of disaffection and general unhappiness. Everybody suffers: the owner and overseer because work isn't being done, and the slaves because what you might call the world of reality catches up with their dreams. It doesn't pay."

"If you say so, Mr. Stark."

"I certainly do. Let this one go, Harry, and don't have any truck with slave sellers except at a duly legal auction where there are papers and guarantees about a slave's health and strength."

"Yes, Mr. Stark," the overseer stammered, his sunburned face becoming redder with embarrassment. "I won't let such a thing happen again."

"Fine, fine." Dudley Stark forced a smile. "Don't let it worry you, Fazenda. You can make it right in the morning, I suppose. You've had a hard day, so get some sleep. You don't have to live off the grounds like Joe Everdine did, but that doesn't mean I want to work you like a field-nigger, either. Good night, Harry."

The overseer was startled because Dudley Stark hadn't lost his trigger-thin temper, and he made one more try to do what he thought was right.

"Be a shame to lose this one, Mr. Stark," he said, trying to be gently persuasive. "He's such a big black buck."

"There's really no choice, if you look at it sensi—"

166

Stark, who had turned to go, suddenly wheeled back. "What does this buck look like, did you say?"

"Very big and black as pitch, Mr. Stark. A good worker, or at least he's used to working if you judge by his appearance."

"Tell me the name of the slave who tried lying for him," Dudley Stark said eagerly. "Was it the fat one?"

"Yes, Mr. Stark, it was. Rufus is his name."

"Rufus was always a friend of Hannibal's," Stark mused. "I suppose it's not impossible that Hannibal got himself shanghaied and the people who had him tried to sell him to a new overseer who wants to stay on the job. Where did you say Hanni—this slave is now?"

"He was at the slave pens when I saw him, Mr. Stark."

"Let's go to the slave pens, Fazenda. I'll bring a pistol from my gun collection."

"I can wait here, then," Fazenda said. Like his employer, he had forgotten about getting any rest in what might be an emergency.

"Meet me here in five minutes," Stark said. "Meanwhile, get some rope."

"You mean, to tie up this nigger?"

"For a start, we'll probably have to tie him up," Dudley Stark said grimly. "Let's be quick, Fazenda. I don't want him having any more chances to get away."

CHAPTER 17

Hannibal had slept and wakened and slept again. When he awoke this time, the sun was coming down and he knew that the slaves would be returning from their day's toil. He would get away as soon as he was able to.

It took time before he was able to stand up, but he realized now that he was weak and dizzy because he hadn't eaten and not because he was sick. He still felt as if somebody was hammering at the top of his head, but it wasn't the way it had been during the day.

He left the small and rickety building, then decided to make for the clearing of trees. He would be safe there for a while. If any slave couple was going to make love, they weren't likely to do it till supper was over. It always surprised Hannibal that after a day in the fields he or any other slave could make love, but he guessed that the need for a woman didn't go away after backbreaking work.

He had been away from slave pens for a while, so he realized how badly they smelled and what a bad way it was for people to live. He hadn't thought of it before, but he knew now that he wasn't ever again going to be a slave. He didn't care if his neck did get stretched.

He supposed that if he lived long enough and got older in the North, where he could be free, he'd be like a lot of older people and long for the days when he was young. But he, Hannibal, wouldn't long for slavery.

He staggered up and out of the cabin and over towards

168

the clearing at last, going through the grove of trees and trying to figure out how he would leave. He didn't expect to see another black man in the clearing at this time, and he drew back when he did see a black man sitting there.

The first sight of that bulging figure told him he was looking at Rufus, but such a Rufus as he had never seen before and, half-amused, hoped he would never see again. The fat slave had tried to smooth his shirt and pants, and rub stains off them. He had wet his hair and doused his face, but not dried them completely. He was grinning and self-satisfied.

His grin at Hannibal was choked off. He jumped up. "You got to get out of here."

"That's what I aim to do," Hannibal agreed. "Glad I saw you, though. I was hoping you might fetch me some grub."

"Don't stand here," Rufus said, probably not having heard Hannibal's last remark. "Go over to the next stand of trees."

"There's hardly any room between 'em," Hannibal protested. "You know the way it is over there."

"Don't stay here," Rufus said, whispering urgently. "I'm seeing Sarah Jane here and I don't want her to see you."

"Sarah Jane? Well, that's good news." Hannibal started for the crowded cluster of trees, speaking over a shoulder with an agreeable lie. "I always did think Sarah Jane liked you."

Rufus said bitterly, "It's not that she gives a hoot about me, just that she wants to know where you are. I said I'd tell her and she said she'd give me a good time if I do."

If Hannibal's guess meant anything, then neither one would get much out of their time together. It was no business of his, though.

"I'm hungry and I need something to eat," he said. "I

169

was telling you that before, but I don't suppose you heard."

"Don't talk so loud, please." Rufus cringed. "All right, I'll get you something, Hannibal. I'll do it as soon as possible. If Sarah does show up, try not to let her see you."

"Don't worry about that." Hannibal wanted no more of Sarah Jane's jealousy.

"Please Hannibal," Rufus whispered. "Not so loud."

Hannibal went on tiptoes to his new hiding place. The trees at this point grew so thickly together that it was nearly impossible for him to stand without having to turn his head to look out. At least he wasn't going to fall in a faint because there wouldn't be any room for him to fall.

Sarah Jane was thoughtful as she finished a supper of chicken bones with a little meat on them, and some spring water. What bothered her was that she had promised to go out and see Rufus at a time when he couldn't possibly tell her anything about Hannibal. After all, Hannibal couldn't be here at the plantation. If he was, he'd be hanged.

What she'd have to do was simply to forget about Hannibal. As far as she was concerned, he didn't exist any longer.

With that decision made, she went to find Samson, who had just finished supper. Samson had been a slave here for as long as he could remember. He was no Hannibal for size and he wasn't nearly as good as Hannibal in the hay, but he was kind and a gal could count on him. He grinned up at her.

"You in the mood for a little storytelling tonight, gal?" he asked.

"One or two stories, maybe."

"After last night's session I couldn't tell you more than one or two stories."

"Let's got to our place."

170

"Okay." Samson chuckled. "How 'bout the big trees?"

"Sure, honey. I like to stand when you're telling stories."

"Okay, Sarah Jane, gal. I've got the same stories I always had, but they always go over big."

"I remember that, honey."

Hannibal heard a man and a woman coming toward the stand of big trees. They had circled the clearing, and he didn't doubt that he'd be seen if Rufus came after him over to this stand of trees. Hannibal took the chance to go to the clearing. Rufus would surely stop off there in order to find out if his gal had come to see him.

He was sure he wasn't overheard. The couple in the trees whispered to each other and there was a rustle of clothes. By the time he got to the clearing, though, he didn't hear a sound; and was sure he was safe.

It took a moment before he changed his mind. No, he wasn't at all safe. He was looking directly at a grinning advancing and lovely Leola.

"I knew you'd be in the place where we made love before, darling," she said quietly as she came towards him. "And I knew you'd come back for me."

Hannibal blinked very quickly. He wasn't dizzy any more, only hungry for food. He knew as well as he could know anything that the next few moments might destroy him no matter what he did. If he moved away, Leola could set up a yell. If he tried to touch her, she could later claim that he had done even worse to her. And if he stayed where he was, her very talk might well bring people to this place.

Come to think of it, he could hear some slaves moving around restlessly nearby.

His eyes must have bulged fearfully, but he was too frightened to move any other part of himself, let alone his entire body. He knew that the next few minutes had to be among the most important of his life.

171

"Don't you remember?" she started sweetly. "Well, I'll help you remember."

And then the fool girl did something so astonishing that Hannibal felt he had to stay rooted to the spot. She approached him, lifted his hands and brought them up to her breasts. His fingers started to tingle and he let out a small moan. Desire for the girl had damnably got to him.

Leola giggled. "You want me, Hannibal. Touch me here . . . and here . . . and *here,* down here . . . ooh, that feels wonderful, just wonderful."

She let his hands fall down to his sides. He made no move towards her. For once in her life, Leola looked puzzled.

"Was that enough, Hannibal? Don't you want to get more excited?"

She was wearing a green dress with black at the throat. Now, as Hannibal watched, she reached for the dress and began to ease it off her body. The dress slithered like a snake and made small crackling sounds as it moved with a life of its own. Her body moved from side to side as well, so that even in the near darkness he could see the play of muscles on this girl's beautiful white body.

The body, that was, as seen through yards of petticoats that rustled and fairly breathed with her. Hannibal tried to make himself turn away, but couldn't. He was going to be in thrall forever to the sight before him. It was as bad as killing himself to keep looking, and yet that was what he did.

Leola Stark reached for the top petticoat and played with buttons before easing them out of the buttonholes and beginning to shrug the first of the petticoats off her body.

What happened then was so quick that he hardly realized all its meaning at the time. What he did know was that in some way he had been responsible for it all.

For the first time he made a sound through his lips as

if begging for mercy, as if begging her not to torture him in this special and painful and horribly delicious way.

From just beyond the clearing he heard what he guessed was an answering snort, and then the heavy figure of Rufus stepped between a pair of big trees and into the clearing.

The fat slave was carrying a package of food for Hannibal, but at the sight of Leola Stark in near undress, the sexually frustrated slave dropped the package. Without any hesitation or any other thought except to satisfy himself instantly, Rufus ran to Leola Stark and gripped her by the shoulders. Then he whirled her around and threw her down to the earth. In a moment he had lowered himself so that his heavy, straining body was on top of the white girl's.

Before anything could be done to stop her, Leola Stark had let out a scream.

When Harry Fazenda came back to the point at which he was supposed to meet his boss, he was carrying a rope. As far as he could tell, he was on time. Dudley Stark hadn't got back to the place with his pistol, not yet.

Actually Stark was in the gun room and trying to find ammunition for his favorite pistol. He hadn't taken much time as yet, heaven knew. It was just that he didn't want to go into the slave pens at night with any pistol except his favorite.

Dudley heard a woman's scream in the direction of the slave pens, and supposed it was one of the darkie gals having a rough time with a persistent boy out there. Negroes were like children, and if they couldn't get just what they wanted they were willing to fight for it.

Harry Fazenda heard the scream, too. If he had been at his own cabin and taking things easy, he would probably have shrugged it off. But as he was in the open air and ready to charge into the slave pens, he decided to

173

run over first and check into the reason for this disturbance. Something in the nature of the voice had made him uneasy. It was too high, too shrill, too genuinely threaded with fear to belong to any of the nigger gals he had seen and talked to.

Irritated, his skin tingling with a sensation he couldn't define, Harry Fazenda started out by himself for the scene of the disturbance.

Dudley Stark had finally found the ammunition for his best pistol. Now, with the pistol in a holster, he stepped into the hallway to join his foreman downstairs.

Before he had taken half a dozen noisy steps, he heard his wife call out, "Did you hear that, Dudley?"

"Hear what?" He was distracted.

"That scream a little while ago."

"Scream? Oh, that. It was coming from the nigger pens. Couldn't be important."

"I almost thought it sounded like Leola."

Dudley snorted. "If all you've got time to do is to have nightmares, then go ahead and do it. But don't keep a man from doing what's really important."

"I don't understand what you mean."

He turned toward the rear of the house, from which the sound of his wife's disembodied voice had come. He felt almost as if she was in the hallway and next to him.

"When I get back to this house again, there'll be one dead slave at Safe Harbor."

Sarah Jane and her boyfriend, Samson, had been at an awkward moment when the scream ripped out fairly close to where they were standing. It was Sarah Jane, ruthlessly practical as always, who moved away first, leaving a stricken Samson.

"Put that thing back in your pants and let's us move," Sarah Jane whispered.

"But—but you can't do this!" Samson gasped.

174

"I can do anything if it means not staying where trouble is," Sarah Jane whispered as she patted her dress back into place. "Come on, boy. Let's be missing."

Nettie had knocked gently on her daughter's room. There was no response. Softly, she opened the door. Her daughter's bed hadn't been slept in.

A search of the house, done as quickly as she could manage, soon convinced her that Leola was nowhere to be seen. Nettie was older than her daughter, of course, and her lungs didn't have as much power as Leola's, but she let out a powerful scream of her own.

By that time, however, her husband was too far away to hear. When one of the house slaves came running in to find out what was wrong, Nettie stared.

"What do you want?"

"To find out if you're all right, ma'am."

"Get out of here. I never want to see you again."

The house slave left the drawing room, puzzled and suddenly worried about being put back into field work again for no known reason.

CHAPTER 18

To Hannibal, the second in which Leola's scream tore out on the humid night air would forever be remembered as the worst moment of his life. He had allowed himself to be trapped and destroyed by lust combined with hunger. No matter what he did now, there would be witnesses.

He could hear the sound of running feet over and above Leola's scream. The very leaves might well have been shivering in horror.

Fat Rufus was tearing Leola's petticoats when Hannibal finally roused himself to interfere. He circled Rufus, getting to the back, then tried to lift him by the midriff. It wouldn't work. In his frustration-fed fury, Rufus kicked out effectively at Hannibal.

It was impossible to grab Rufus by the hair. Only one course remained open to him. He forced Rufus' head around, then kicked him in the chin. Rufus' head jerked back and the eyes shut tightly. He wasn't conscious any longer, but the full weight of his body rested on Leola. She was gasping now along with her screams.

Hannibal had to take time to ease the body off Leola or she would have been squashed to death. It was more time than he ought to have taken. He ought to have run with every ounce of breath that was in him.

Just as Rufus' body thudded to earth, a Negro said loudly: "What are you doing here?"

Hannibal whirled to face a hard and muscular slave

176

named Tyler, a slave with whom he had fought on dozens of occasions. The two men had eventually reached a wary truce, a knife-edged truce that could be broken at any moment. Tyler had wanted Sarah Jane before Hannibal got her and he had tried to make a play for Miriam shortly after she had decided that Hannibal was the only man in the world for her.

Behind Tyler, three other slaves stood. The three were friends of his. They did many things together and formed a private association among themselves. Nobody except their friends liked any of them, and their meanness was a by-word in the slave pens.

Swiftly, each of the men looked at the form of Leola Stark lying on the earth.

Tyler ran his tongue over his cracked lips. "It's our turn now."

Hannibal was amazed. "Do you know who she is, you fool? You'll get all our necks stretched."

Tyler was startled. "Hannibal?"

"Yes."

Tyler paused and then, maddened, said, "We go to the well and then we bury her when it's over. Get out of my way now, boy, if you know what's good for you."

"Won't." Hannibal glanced at Leola. "Run if you know what's good for you. I'll try and keep them here."

Leola tried to get up, but she felt as if every bone in her body had been broken. She gasped and gritted her teeth in trying to get up.

"She ain't really moving 'cause she wants it," Tyler grinned. "She likes a black hickey up her road. Don't you, gal? Out the way, Hannibal."

"Try and get me out the way."

Tyler spoke to the other three slaves. "Finish him off."

One of the slaves ran the width of this clearing, bringing him to a point behind Hannibal. The others advanced from two sides. Tyler skirted one of them, cutting short his path to Leola.

177

That was the moment when Harry Fazenda crashed through the clearing.

"Stand still every one of you," the overseer shouted, "or I'll flog the eyes right out of your heads."

Dudley Stark reached the meeting point and felt sure that his overseer hadn't yet arrived. He cursed, but decided against wasting time. A wagon was handy, but no fresh horse was nearby. He had to run to the stables to get a fresh horse. It was true that the stench of horse would make it impossible to wear his present clothes again until they had been washed and laundered, but he couldn't have cared less about that.

On his way to the slave pens, with nothing to do except spur the horse onward, he noticed again how beautiful the night was and how well the weather had been holding up. The land was his, the slaves worked for him. He had money and position and a good family. This was a fine way of life indeed, and no meddlers in Washington were ever going to take it away from him.

A hundred yards in front of the slave pens Dudley got off the horse, whispered gently to it, and then hurried toward the slave pens. For the first time and over the sound of the horse gulping for breath, Dudley was aware of noise, of shouts and even of screams. He stopped, never having heard such sounds from the slave pens before. He gripped the wooden stock of his pistol.

The commotion was coming from beyond a cluster of trees. Slaves were running back and forth and shouting:

"I'll kill 'em, kill 'em every one."

"Kill the whites, kill 'em."

Dudley Stark decided against firing in air. He supposed that Hannibal had roused the other slaves to a pitch of fury and wouldn't fire unless he had to.

But where on earth was Harry Fazenda? What could have happened to him?

The three marauding slaves, halted in their plan to destroy Hannibal while Tyler took the first turn with their master's daughter, whirled around on Fazenda.

The overseer realized now that he was seeing something new to him: he was seeing slaves maddened with lust and afraid of no man. He had looked only long enough to recognize Miss Leola on the earth and out of his reach. He couldn't get close enough to help her.

He realized, too, that he carried a rope in his hand, and no other weapon. Not even a lion trainer at the circus could have handled these animals.

The three slaves turned on Fazenda, slowly coming towards him. The white overseer blanched. He took a step backwards, which was too dangerous.

Tyler ordered, "Kill him."

It was said quietly. Three other slaves advanced on Fazenda, now. The white overseer raised the rope, but it didn't keep the blacks away and it didn't give him the freedom of movement that he needed, either. He would have been better off to throw the rope away and use his fists instead.

One of the slaves kicked him in the stomach. When Fazenda bent over swiftly in his sickness, another slave drew out a knife and cut him in the neck. A red smile of blood appeared obscenely on Harry Fazenda's broad neck.

The slaves worked quickly. The rope disappeared, and Fazenda's clothes were taken off him. The body was naked. One of the slaves reached out a knife for the dead man's sex organs. The knife moved slowly. Blood drops appeared on the dead thighs and lower stomach. . . .

The fight between the three men and Fazenda had left Hannibal to confront Tyler and nobody else. Hannibal acted swiftly, drawing up a hand on Tyler's mouth so that his friends wouldn't hear and then turning Tyler around and trying to bend the body backwards as if wanting to snap it.

179

Tyler was unexpectedly strong. He kicked out at Hannibal, hurting him once. The next time his kick passed harmlessly. Leola, whose screams had been the only loud noise in this clearing, suddenly stood up, shaky and surprised that she was able to do it. She wanted nothing more now than to run for home, to be back in her good and soft bed. Not if she lived to be a hundred would she ever forget that fat beast of a nigger on top of her.

Almost as if he had known that she was thinking about him, Rufus stirred.

The fat man, slightly recovered from the beating he had taken, and as determined as he was groggy, opened his bleary eyes on the sight of Leola Stark shivering in her petticoats—and nearly lost his mind once more.

He tried to stand up, swaying groggily. From back of him he could hear other slaves shouting that the overseer was dead and now was the time to kill all the whites.

"Kill 'em all, you hear?"

Somebody screamed.

"Don't leave any whites alive—not one."

Rufus trying to get to his feet was the one sight that could galvanize Leola. She cowered behind Hannibal, who had kept on fighting Tyler. There was a snapping sound in front of her, a sound of breaking like nothing she had ever heard before, and Hannibal let Tyler down gently to the earth.

Through chattering teeth Leola said, "I'm going."

"Where?" That was Hannibal, his voice hoarse with recent exertion.

"Home."

She was close to losing all her control. Didn't he understand what she wanted now, what she needed? Hadn't he been brought up with a family?

"You can't get past them," Hannibal said, meaning the three slaves who were watching one of them use the knife on the lower part of Harry Fazenda's dead body.

A friend of Tyler's said, "Cut real careful and get it just right."

He turned around, either having sensed that Hannibal had pointed in his general direction or wanting to take some pleasure in the sight of Tyler humiliating a wealthy white girl. He saw Tyler lying on the earth, alone, unmistakably dead. He saw Rufus trying to get up.

Swiftly the slave friend of Tyler's whirled on Hannibal, but spoke to his friend. "Give me that knife. I've got some business here."

Leola gasped.

Hannibal talked to her, but looked straight ahead of him at the slave getting the knife. "You can't go home now. The only chance for you is to come with me."

"All right, all right." Leola's voice was rising threateningly. "Anything at all, but let's go."

Hannibal scooped up the girl's dress and took her by the arm. As they started out of the clearing, Hannibal walking behind her, the slave who had been handed the knife made a rush for him.

Hannibal could have handled him, but didn't have to. Rufus, trying to catch his balance, blundered in front of the slave. The knife rose angrily, then fell. Rufus gasped. Blood drenched his clothes. His eyes were shut now. He swayed, the bigness of his body keeping the killer slave moving forward. The slave tried to push the body out of the way but couldn't. He used the knife again, then, as Hannibal and the girl disappeared out the far end of the clearing. He cursed and ran around the heavy slave's body at last.

"Forget them," one of the others said. "Let's us kill whites."

"Yes, kill the whites, all of 'em."

Shouting and maddened, the slaves stumbled out of the clearing.

CHAPTER 19

Dudley Stark, who had heard the shouts and was looking at blood lust shining in his slaves' faces, knew very well that these three had to be stopped. The message could hardly have been more clear. He thanked his lucky stars that he was carrying the pistol, and drew it into a hand.

It was cocked and ready as he rose from his hiding place, having decided to try stopping these slaves by giving commands rather than using gunplay. After all, bullets were valuable and so were slaves. Unless he had to do it, why should he use a small property to destroy a large one?

"Stop it, you boys," he called. "Stop or I'll shoot."

They saw him at last. One of them was holding the sort of rope that Dudley would have expected Fazenda to be carrying. For the first time it seriously occurred to Dudley that his overseer might have come to harm at the hands of those boys, and that the situation was even more serious than he had been considering it to be.

The second of the three slaves was holding something in one closed hand. The third one carried a knife.

The knife-wielder made one move toward Stark and never again did anything else that mattered. Stark shot him. The noise was so loud it caused Stark himself to wince. Puffs of smoke hung in the humid air. The knife-wielder dropped his weapon, gasped and fell.

"You other two, come over here and—"

Dudley Stark couldn't hear himself talk on account of

182

that noise of the pistol shot. The slave with the rope suddenly ran off. The other one, who had been carrying something in a closed hand, stared wildly at Dudley Stark and then opened the hand and threw its contents at Dudley Stark's face.

The slave ran off before whatever-it-was struck Dudley Stark, in the nose as it happened and not too heavily, then landed on the grassy earth below him. Dudley Stark had felt sick when the object struck him but when the moon shone on it as it lay in the grass, he became queasy. He couldn't help turning away, bending over and throwing up. The warm semiliquid flooded from his opened mouth. It stopped in time, leaving him hollow and weak. His mouth was filled with a taste that reminded him of grapeshot. He had to lean against a tree, shaking as he tried to recover himself, knowing he was giving up valuable time but not able to do anything else. For he knew very well that he had been hit in the face with Harry Fazenda's cut-off testicles.

"Kill the whites!"
"Kill every one of 'em!"
"Don't let 'em stay alive!"
"That's right, kill 'em, every one!"
The cry had been taken up by others, and it sounded in the night and echoed through the hills.

Bolivar grinned. He had been a slave at Safe Harbor for a long time, and he had generally been well behaved. Only once, for example, had he been flogged. He never took advantage of any other slaves, boys or gals. He was a cheerful fellow, as far as everybody was concerned, and if he had any hates he kept them to himself instead of making them the business of anybody else.

His only real hate at the moment was this young kid called Samson. Him and Sarah Jane were always loving it up somewhere or other, and the notion of it made Bolivar sick. Not that Bolivar had ever asked Sarah Jane to so much as go walking with him or that he particularly liked her for that matter. She was thin, and those titties of hers looked ugly through the dress she wore. No, being with men was good enough for Bolivar.

But he always had the feeling that he was missing something important. Whenever he saw the scrawny Samson he looked at him smiling secretly at Sarah Jane and thought that Samson was doing something that would be fine to do and he hated the idea that a thin fool of a slave was doing it while he himself did nothing like that at all.

Bolivar heard the call, "Kill whites," and nodded and picked it up and yelled and cheered.

Somebody in the slave pens shouted, "The main house! Let's go to the main house and do it there!"

Bolivar echoed that call, too. A group of slaves, who had been laying around spiritlessly, had suddenly jumped to their feet. They shouted and cheered in spite of bone-tiredness.

With the others, Bolivar ran out of the slave pens. Everybody was headed for the big house, swaying almost drunkenly in their new and cheerful arrogance.

Bolivar, pausing to let the others out of the dirty old house that passed for the slave pen, saw Sarah Jane hand-in-hand with her Samson as they returned to the slave area. Samson drew his hand out of hers. Sarah Jane argued with him.

Samson's voice rose and he said sharply, "I'm going out with the others. I want to kill me some whites like they want to kill themselves some niggers."

Bolivar grunted, his hands working in and out. It wasn't fair that here was the only good time he'd ever had in his life and that damned Samson was going to be part of it, too. Was there any pleasure that Samson didn't have?

Well, Samson wouldn't get this pleasure. Almost without knowing what he was doing, Bolivar took three steps toward Samson and wrapped both hands around Samson's scrawny throat. Samson started to yell, but couldn't keep it up for long.

Sarah Jane called out, "Have you gone crazy, boy?" She pounded the back of Bolivar's neck with a closed fist, which hurt but didn't stop him.

Samson's body went limp as the life left it.

Bolivar stepped away from Samson, then, letting the body fall. Sarah Jane was still pounding the back of Bolivar's neck.

He reached behind him, holding the hands, and pulled the gal's body tightly against his. Sarah Jane called out, cursed, and finally leaned over and bit him on an ear.

Bolivar gasped and let the gal go. As he turned she kicked him just above a kneecap. Bolivar reached out a hand that he had made into a fist and laid it across Sarah Jane's jaw. Sarah Jane folded up and hit the earth next to her dead lover.

Bolivar hesitated, waiting to pull up her dress and see what lay between the tops of her thighs. Sarah Jane was so domineering it might not have surprised him to find a man's tools there.

All around him the cry echoed, "Kill . . . kill . . . kill whites!"

Maybe it was best to leave the gal like she was and not think too much about her. There would be plenty of time to find out what gals were like. There wasn't so much time to find out how it would be to kill himself a white man—or a white woman, like Miss Leola.

So he joined the others on his way to the main house. There was a smell in the air that reminded him of warm food, and it struck him that it was unusually bright outside tonight, but he didn't think of putting the two facts together.

185

Leola looked up at Hannibal and said proudly, "We did it, all right."

"Yes," Hannibal agreed. He rolled his body away from hers. They had been in a grassy glade together, partly at her insistence but mostly at his. Now that it was over, sharp pangs of hunger had begun to assail Hannibal once again.

"I have to get something to eat."

Leola pouted. "I'll bet all men are like that. First they have their way with a woman and then they think about any other things."

"You wanted it as much as I did," Hannibal pointed out, perhaps rightly.

"We both wanted it," Leola agreed.

He nodded. Never would he tell her that it hadn't been as good for him as he had hoped. There was the extra edge, of course, that he was with a white gal and he could be hanged if he was found out, hanged without anybody feeling doubts afterwards. That had given the few moments with her a sauce of danger and a feeling of sinfulness. Which was good, of course, as far as it went.

Leola hadn't been that good a partner in sex, though. She didn't really know a lot of the things that a gal is supposed to do in order to make a man happy. She didn't have any feeling for getting a man worked up once the two of them were flat together. It seemed odd that he should have spent a lot of time as a kid thinking about how wonderful it would be if he could shove his thing in a white gal; and when the time came the white gal turned out not to be very good in the hay.

Besides he kept remembering Cindy and how she liked it with him and how good she was when it came to doing these things together.

As for Leola, she was hurt and confused as well as tired. She had expected that being with a man would be like going to paradise, but all it happened to be was a lot

186

of discomfort and humiliation and irritation. She felt as if she had been torn apart.

Hannibal got to his feet, and stood in the direction of Safe Harbor. He turned quickly after one look and then helped Leola up, standing in such a way that she wouldn't be able to see back of her in the direction of the plantation.

She tried to look around him, but he drew an arm across her waist, knowing he was taking an extra risk with his life in case anybody should see the two of them, but doing it anyway in order to keep the gal from being badly shaken up.

Leola asked him, "What is it that I could see from here and you don't want me to see?"

"Nothing much," he answered roughly. "Just that there's no time to lose and we better go as far away from there as we can get and do it now. I'm trying to get you to move on."

She nodded. Hannibal walked behind her. As he moved, his eyes caught something that might be a loaf of bread. Believing in miracles for a moment, he bent over.

There was a small sized rock that could serve as a platform in front of Leola. Swiftly she stood on it, turned around, looked back in the direction of Safe Harbor, and stepped down again.

She was walking again as Hannibal stood up, empty-handed. He had gone out of the way to keep her from hearing bad news, and now she would let him be content in feeling sure that he had succeeded. She wouldn't throw a tantrum, even as frightened as she had become.

She walked ahead bravely, chin up, shoulders back.

Hannibal knew that if the girl had looked back she would have crumpled up. Like the girl, walking ahead quietly, he felt satisfied with himself.

CHAPTER 20

Dudley Stark, the great waves of weakness having passed over him at last, stood up straight for the first time in a long while. He glanced toward the trees, certain that beyond them lay the nude violated body of the overseer. Then he looked away, trying to forget about everything except what would need to be done now in the shortest possible time.

In the distance he could hear the calls, "Kill whites," and "Kill every one of 'em."

Somebody else shouted, "To the big house . . . the big house!"

Dudley Stark straightened himself. If they were going to be at one place, then it would be easier to round them up. Of course his wife and daughter were there and he saw no sense in denying to himself that there might well be some bad trouble here. He could only hope that he'd get back in time to save the lives of his wife and daughter. If it was necessary, he'd kill off every piece of living property he owned.

He took a lurching step in the direction of the main house, straightened himself, and then began to run. It was not only necessary for him to run, but it was easier for him than walking would have been.

Annette Stark, who was called Nettie, wasn't generally the sort of woman who worried about problems. Leola might not have been in her room, but she must be close

188

by. Until it was known that Leola had come to harm or done anything bad, there was no sensible reason for worrying that Nettie Stark could figure out.

Nettie hadn't always been so placid. As a child, she had been subject to tantrums that put Leola's temper in the shade. Nettie's mother had paid for the services of a hypnotist to show Nettie how to relax. Nettie had been interested and curious at the notion, but she nearly collapsed with laughter at sight of the hypnotist.

He had been a seedy-looking, definitely down-at-heels type who worked in carnivals. The idea of learning anything from him was ridiculous. How could somebody as rich as Nettie learn anything from an old man who was poor?

Nevertheless the hypnotist had tried to earn his fee. In the presence of Nettie's folks he had tried to get her to relax. He told her sit down and put her feet flat on the floor, then close her eyes and try to imagine one part of the body after another in a state of calm. "Now the soles of your feet are asleep . . . think of them sleeping, the left foot and then the right foot . . . now your thighs are asleep . . ."

Nettie would never tell her parents why she laughed when the demonstration was done and a failure; but actually it was because the hypnotist had never mentioned any private parts of the body.

Nettie didn't relax at all, but the others in her family practiced it on their own and became proud of their achievement. Nettie became a rambunctious young woman, but her folks became placid enough to leave her alone when she was running wild.

Only during her Grand Tour of Europe had she come into contact with the method of relaxing once again. One of the girls taking the tour with her had fallen ill with a fit of the vapors when they were at a British seaside resort called Bournemouth—or was it Brighton? At any rate, an influential doctor who charged many guineas for

189

each visit had persuaded Nettie's touring companion to relax in the very same way that the seedy-looking hypnotist had used. The friend was too jittery to relax, but for Nettie the method now began to work very well. She always claimed from then on that it accounted for her sleeping as well as she did.

With Leola gone, Nettie tried to keep herself from worrying as much as a different mother might do. She had decided in her time-proved way to relax. Not for a moment did she doubt that Leola would be back. After all, this business about Leola developing such a great affection for a slave, if you please, hardly made any sense at all. Not to a person who knew the self-centered Leola at all well.

Come to think of it, Nettie could remember as a young lady that her father had once bought a handsome slave named Richelieu. How many times young Nettie had imagined Richelieu's skin next to hers, imagined him touching her in the most exciting places! But in her case it hadn't gone any further than that. With an impetuous child like Leola there was always the problem that she might push it further of her own free will.

She wouldn't deny (seriously, now!) that there could very well be something to all the difficulty. With one woman's skeptical point of view about another, Nettie admitted that it was very possible indeed.

But it didn't follow that her daughter had gone off to be with the slave, had actually run away from her own home. Leola would be back soon enough, and there would be some foolish explanation for the whole matter of her absence for a short while.

Nettie sat with feet on the floor and started to relax herself. Now the soles of the feet were asleep, now the thighs were asleep . . .

She was up to the stomach when she heard a scrabbling sound on the lower level and at the front door. It was Leola, of course. Nettie decided to wait in the draw-

190

ing room, which her daughter would have to pass in order to go upstairs. Nettie would speak to her daughter for a few moments, for the child's own good, to be sure.

The downstairs noise sounded extraordinary, almost as if Leola was trying to crash the door. Was it possible that her daughter might have taken more liquor than she could hold? Certainly that was the way she sounded.

Instead of only lecturing the girl, Nettie decided that Leola would really be hauled over the coals. This was not a trivial matter, although drunkenness would be easier to control than any situation in which she had done harm to herself by indulging her body with that of a slave.

Nettie stood up and started down the stairs, which faced the front entrance. She was in time to see that the door had indeed been crashed open, and to see a dozen colored men and a few women standing defiantly in the doorway. Nettie supposed that they were plantation slaves, but she had never seen any slaves looking at her with the combination of fear and hatred on these black faces below her.

Her own face rigid, she asked, "Why are you here? What do you want?"

One of the girls cackled, "We want everything you've got, old woman."

The others laughed and surged into the hall. Nettie realized that nothing she said would have any effect whatever on these animals.

"My, it smell funny!"

"Look at that!"

"I don't like it. Break it!"

"Like this?"

"Harder. It don't work that way."

"Take one of them with you for the slave pens. We could use 'em."

"You must be funning! We ain't never gonna see the insides of no slave pens again, one way or the other."

191

"If that's right, then break it."

"Like this?"

"Sure."

"What are you doing over there?"

"Thought I'd leave some recollection that I was here."

"Pissing on the floor? Is that your idea of a recollection?"

"Good enough for them."

"You ought to be hanged first and flogged later, if anybody asks me."

"Nobody's asking. You try it yourself, big man. It's fun to see how your piss goes all over the room. You might think the floor is straight—it looks straight—but it's built on a hill, I swear."

"Say, you know something? You're right."

Nettie had declined to retreat. Not an inch backwards would she go while these animals rampaged on her property. She only hoped that Leola had gone away and was with her slave after all. Nothing else but this could have made her hope so.

Some of the animals—Nettie wouldn't think of them as human beings—talked mockingly to her.

"You like this thing, old woman? Nice, isn't it? Well, there it goes."

"Dropped it, didn't he? We flog him without mercy for that, old woman. We hang him by the balls."

"You know what balls are, old woman?"

"She knows, she knows."

They had made their voices lower for a while in imitation of a white man's, and the voices were taut with imitated anger as well as the real thing.

"Hey! Where you going, old woman?"

For Nettie had suddenly vanished swiftly up the stairs. She could hear the crashing of antiques and the loud talk over the grating noises.

"It don't matter where she goes. She won't get far!"

"We'll take care of her."

"Yes, we will!"

Nettie had hurried upstairs and to her room. She picked up the kerosene lamp, turned on her heels and started back again. She drew a deep breath before reaching the stairs. She might have turned or tried to leave the house by one of the back entrances, but she wouldn't show any of those animals for even a moment that she was afraid of them.

Lamp in hand, she started down. Her first impression was that many more slaves had come into the hallways downstairs and fanned out through the lower part of the house. She could hear furniture being smashed along with various fragile items which she had always been proud to own. There was an odious smell in the house and she didn't doubt that at least a few of the slaves had moved their bowels on the floor of the main house.

One of the animals saw her, pointed up and called:

"There she is, the old woman."

"She's carrying a lamp," somebody else whispered.

"What for you carrying that lamp, old woman?"

"Fire," the same person whispered. "She gonna set us on fire. She gonna roast us all."

"And herself with it."

"Whites can't get hurt by fire," somebody else snorted. "Any fool knows that."

"We'll fix her. Go after her, you!"

"Go after her yourself. You're so smart, always telling other people what to do. Go after her yourself, 'masta'."

"Think I'm afraid of old white woman?"

"You might not be 'fraid, but you're here and she's up there."

"I haven't got anything to calm her down with."

"Think she'll beat you up?"

"I don't want to put my hands on her less I have to."

"Get the rope."

"What rope?"

"Somebody took a rope off that white bastard before. Get the rope and tie her up."

"Where's the rope? Who's got the rope? Anybody?"

"Get the rope!"

"Here it is."

And all this time, Nettie could hear the same sounds and smell the same vileness as before.

"Up there! She's right up there, old white woman with the lamp. Tie her up."

"Do better than that. Get into her."

That call had come from somebody out of sight, but the cry caught on.

"Who wants an old woman?"

"Get into her, get in, get in!"

Handclapping had started up, and slaves were clustering in the hallway as if for a celebration. The slave carrying the rope, his eyes squeezed half-shut and moving carefully, started up the stairs.

Nettie could no longer bring herself to hesitate. She whipped the glass against the railing, sending it into flying shards. One of the small shards landed in her left eye. She called out with pain that the slaves thought was fear. They laughed and cheered.

The fire reached the stairs and descended toward the Negroes in the hallway, while other flames started on the red path of destruction upwards.

"Get her for that! Don't let her away!"

"Burn her! See if her hand takes the fire or not. Let's find out how much a white woman can really take."

Nettie heard, but she felt only the pain in her eye. She was fortunate that there was so much pain there that she hardly felt the agony and humiliation as a black man tore the clothes off her from the bottom and began to mutilate her. She cried out. Nor did she see other slaves practically risk their lives by climbing up the stairs to take her.

194

The smoke smell blotted out some of the others and the crash of furniture wasn't so loud. Her back was beginning to pain her at the middle and across. By comparison with the other pains, what was happening in front of her was far away and almost as if in somebody else's nightmare.

Above her, she heard a voice: "What are you doing here, 'Tilda?"

And a woman cackled, "I want my share."

"I always knew you was as queer as wooden cotton, gal."

And a moment of humiliation not like the other, with no physical pain for her but in another way so much worse. Nettie gasped and cried in her vain efforts to reach out against somebody, to hurt one of the animals destroying her.

The inferno of smoke sent stair rails crashing and toppled her to the ground. She felt certain this time that her back had been broken. The milling around and screaming on all sides of her would always be unbelievable. Every part of her body was disturbed now and would be disturbed no matter how long she lived.

A black hand was fondling her dried-up breasts almost as if the breasts had belonged to a young girl.

She was a young girl again and Richelieu had come to her. Wasn't this Richelieu, even though his hands were rough and his body that of a tiger? He was ferocious indeed, her Richelieu. Why had she waited so long for him?

The flames mounted higher, the screams became louder, the stench and shouts were unbearable. There was pain all through her body. Flames had reached the ceiling.

The chandelier, which had been a set-piece for years, quivered and fell. She saw it coming and prayed it would cut her life off. For once she was lucky.

The screaming had started again, higher pitched. "I'm getting out here, out of here."

It was a friend of Tyler's who whirled to the door and started out. The noise that popped next was loud, but only the slaves closest to the door heard it. Tyler's friend wheeled around, a look of pain on his face. He collapsed and was dead before he hit the burning floor.

One of the slaves shrieked, "Oh God, Master Dudley is out there and waiting for us."

PART FOUR

CHAPTER 21

"I'm hungry," Leola said.

Hannibal, who was famished, felt sorry for her and told himself at the same time that it would be good for Leola to want something she couldn't get right away. All his life that he could remember he had wanted the freedom he didn't have, not yet.

But he had forgotten for the moment that a white person could always get what she wanted. There was a farmhouse ahead, and Leola stopped at it. The man and woman, named Porter, invited her to have a meal with them. As for Hannibal, they suggested that their own slave couple could put up something for him as soon as they had the time.

The man and woman who were slaves of the Porters were an older couple. The woman, a dried-up creature named Hertha, asked Hannibal questions while he ate.

"You got many slaves at Safe Harbor?"

"Not now." Hannibal thumbed back of him. "If you could look in that direction far enough, you'd see why."

"What do you mean? How do you know if you aren't there?"

"When something happens, it's the colored who die. You know what I mean."

Hertha crossed herself.

"Of course this is strictly between us. I don't want Miss Leola to know."

Hertha looked awed, probably suspecting that Hannibal was gifted with second sight.

Leola had wangled a horse and wagon from the Porters, promising to return it or pay back in kind. She made a point of ordering Hannibal to drive. Hannibal, who had only seen drivers in wagons but had never actually done it himself, found the going harder than he would have expected.

Leola sat behind him, as a mistress was supposed to do when driving with one of her slaves. She touched up her blonde hair as best she was able and murmured about how badly she must have looked. Hannibal was only thinking that as soon as they got to a town he might be able to get himself smuggled up North.

She had been talking and now she suddenly asked, "What do *you* think, Hannibal?"

He said absently, "I wasn't listening."

Leola drew a deep breath of shock, as if she had been betrayed after giving the best years of her life to some ungrateful man. Hannibal started to say he was sorry, but gave up on it. She didn't seem interested in his regrets, only in her injury.

He was feeling grateful when they got to a town at last, but the feeling didn't last long. The town, with its fountain in the center and its small houses around it, was the same one in which he had fought with and killed that white boxer, Quayle, in front of hundreds of other white people.

Leola said, "Ask the directions to a boarding house."

Hannibal whispered, "Not in this town, please."

"There's nothing wrong with Brayton. It's a perfectly good town as far as I know."

He decided it was best not to tell her what he had done in this town.

198

"Stop over there," Leola said. "I'll ask directions. You don't have to talk if you don't want to."

She probably figured that she was offering a compromise because he didn't want to sound like a slave begging for favors from any white. It was true that he didn't, of course, but the real reason for his not wanting to stop was so much more important.

A white man on the corner suggested Mrs. Leach's boarding house, which was two blocks down. The white man didn't seem to have looked at Hannibal, but he said that he wasn't sure if Mrs. Leach would put up any property of the young lady's. Hannibal said nothing, having no part of the talk between two whites about himself.

Mrs. Leach, the boarding house keeper, turned out to be a heavy woman who was friendly and showed her accommodations to Leola. She wouldn't let Hannibal in the house, stopping him with a finger. He had to wait on the grass until the two women returned. Leola looked pleased when she stepped out to the porch.

"I hope you can put up my slave in the stable," she said. "I'll be glad to pay extra, of course."

"I'm afraid that won't do," Mrs. Leach said, her friendliness fading. "I won't put up—well, slaves."

"Not even in a stable?"

"Nowhere on my property, Miss. I'm sorry, but that's a rule of the house."

Hannibal wanted to say that he'd find a room close by. It was the arrangement he would have liked best. In such a case he'd get time to look around for a smuggler who would arrange to get him up North. And he'd be able to spend his free time inside if he figured he had to do that to keep from being recognized by any white man who had seen the fatal fight.

"I'm not asking for anything unreasonable," Leola said.

Mrs. Leach pointed out, "Miss, I'm opposed to slavery.

I'm not a smuggler or anything like that, but I am opposed to it and I will not permit a symbol of slavery under my roof no matter how good a boarding fee it costs me."

Hannibal sighed. The woman was good-hearted, but as a result of it he wasn't likely to find it easy to get a place for the night.

Leola shook her head, every inch the slave owner who was loyal to her own. "I'm afraid I can't agree to such an arrangement, Mrs. Leach. I find your rules quite unrealistic."

"Sorry you're not pleased, Miss Stark."

Between them the women, each in her own way being friendly to him, were making Hannibal's life much harder.

"Can you suggest any who might be more accommodating?" Leola asked.

"You might try the Brattles. They're down the road. He's a shiftless bum and she does most of the work, but I'm sure they'll put you up. Of course the rooms aren't nearly as good as what I'm offering."

Which was probably true, judging from Leola's expression when she came downstairs with Mrs. Brattle, who was the sort of worn-out looking woman who gets a heart attack at forty. Her husband had been sitting in the parlor, feet up, pretending to read a newspaper. He looked exactly like the sort of man who'd have been at that fight such a short time ago, but he didn't seem to have glanced at a slave who was with his mistress. Leola's presence was saving his life in Brayton, he realized.

Leola walked into the parlor first, then sighed and turned mutely to Hannibal, who had been standing quietly and with feet apart.

"The room is adequate, agreed," she said to Mrs. Brattle. "I take it that there will be no difficulty about putting up my slave. In your stable, perhaps."

"We can arrange that," Mrs. Brattle said. She had a weak, whining voice that fit her appearance perfectly.

Brattle put in, "Of course it'll come to a little extra, Miss."

He stood up and bowed to Leola, like the squire of the mansion receiving a titled guest. He was a hefty man with gleaming eyes set in a round face.

His wife sniffed. "Himself over there does all the rate-setting."

Leola said, "I am prepared to pay one dollar a night for myself and twenty-five cents for my slave."

"You're a reasonable wench—ah, woman, I mean," Brattle beamed. He turned to his wife. "Maude, take the lady's effects upstairs. What are you waiting for?"

"I have no effects with me," Leola said. "They shall arrive tomorrow."

"Very well, then," Brattle said, having raised his eyebrows and lowered them again. "Maude, show the nigger where he'll be sleeping."

Hannibal was led out to the stable, which was a small building behind the house. There were two tired looking horses who lived here. Some of the limp straw could be bunched together to make a fair resting place. In the Brattle house, everything looked tired and worn except for Mr. Brattle himself.

Hannibal was fed in the Brattle kitchen. Brattle sat and watched him. He didn't seem to have read another page of the newspaper in his lap. If there was any mention in it of the hunt for a slave named Hannibal or of a fire at Safe Harbor, the fire he had dimly seen, then Brattle wouldn't know anything about it.

He said to Hannibal, "Your mistress is what you'd call —uh, mettlesome."

Hannibal looked up, his eyes narrowed.

"It isn't every young miss who takes a trip with a slave, not in today's South where heaven knows what might

201

happen if you go alone someplace. When I was a lad, we were all of us a lot safer in our beds than we are nowadays."

"That's right, sir." Hannibal gave the idiotically cheerful smile that was expected from a black man talking to a white. "Miss Leola's a fine young woman."

Brattle turned to his newspaper, but couldn't keep his attention on it. He finally said to his wife that he was leaving for a short while.

Hannibal was called up to Leola's room a few moments after he finished dinner. He climbed the creaky old staircase and knocked on the door of her room. Leola admitted him to what he thought was a beautiful room, but she carefully kept the door open.

"Hannibal, what are your plans?" she asked quietly.

He told the truth. "To find somebody who can help me get up North."

"How can you do that?"

"I don't know just yet, but I'll do it."

"Very well. I'll stay here until you've made the plans and then I'll return home." Leola looked sad. "My folks must be wondering what's become of me after the fire."

Hannibal blinked. "Miss?"

"I saw that the house had caught fire," Leola said. "I thought it was best to keep going with you. The slaves were making such a difficulty that I knew I'd be safer this way. I've always felt safe with you."

Hannibal nodded nervously. He wanted to be outside and looking for help, not inside and trying to show a girl how to make love. Not even a white girl.

"If I'm to get help for myself, Miss Leola, there isn't any time to be lost."

"Certainly." She smiled. "Let's go out for a drive, Hannibal. It won't look so suspicious while you're making your contacts as it will if you're in Brayton by yourself."

"That's right, Miss Leola—and thanks."

He had never expected to be thanking a white person

202

for anything and to mean it at the same time, but he did mean it now.

Brattle turned to his wife. "It's been a long day, Maude, and I'm getting to feel it after a day like this."

Mrs. Brattle, who was darning a pair of her husband's socks with the help of needle and thread and upturned shot glass, didn't make any comment.

"You work too hard," Brattle said, shifting in his chair. "Believe me, though, Maude, there'll come a day when we'll be better off by far. A home of our own, and with a few slaves to run things. Not bad, hey, Maude?"

"I don't see what we're going to retire on if I don't keep working," the practical Mrs. Brattle said.

"I keep an eye on the main chance, Maude, as you know," Brattle reminded her, then wriggled in the chair. "I'm surprised you tolerate a window as wide open as that one. It sets the chills on your bones and it might give you the rheum."

Mrs. Brattle complained mildly, "If you want me to close the window, which is right next to yourself, I wish you'd come right out with it and say so."

Over the noise of his wife's closing the window a bit, Brattle said affably, "Why do you think I scan the paper, Maude? Because I'm on the lookout for new opportunities to make us our fortune. All the gold of El Dorado isn't enough for what I want for you, after all the work you've done—for us."

"And your contribution is to look at the paper."

"Certainly." Brattle made a noise of crinkling it. He even glanced down at a news story. "Right here it says that there's a reward of five hundred dollars for information leading to the arrest of the Negro who killed Felix Quayle here in town. Believe me, Maude, that's important to us."

"Are you planning to claim it?"

"I'm in as good a position as anybody else," Brattle

203

said confidently. "I saw that fight, Maude. I was as close to that Negro as—as I am to you. Well; maybe a little further away, but not much."

Mrs. Brattle nodded. "That was the night you were supposed to buy some groceries for us."

"Well, I did it two nights later," Brattle said defensively. "The point is that if the Negro ever crosses my path, Maude, and believe me I'm looking for him, he won't get away from me. That's what I call keeping an eye on the main chance."

"Yes, dear." Maude finished darning the stocking and put away the sewing kit. "You'll excuse me, dear, but I'm going to bed."

"Join you in a little while." Brattle sighed after his wife had gone out of the room. She was a good woman and she worked hard, but he didn't know how he could make believe he was interested in her at all, in the hay. Maude would have been all right if she didn't work so hard, though.

CHAPTER 22

For the first time in this new day, Dudley Stark looked at the damage, or as much of it as he could see. Safe Harbor had been destroyed from main house to slave pens. Fire had eaten the crop. He was a ruined man.

His wife had died in that fire, he was sure, and his daughter as well. He was a man alone.

The slaves he hadn't shot had died inside the house. A number of them had tried to get out the back way when the skeleton of the house caved in on them. Dudley didn't wince when he remembered their screams and he didn't care about the loss of life. He was sorry about the property loss that the deaths of so many slaves added up to, but that was his only regret as far as they were concerned.

Last night, a pair of neighbors had come riding up with shotguns at the ready. They couldn't help in any way except to put him up overnight, and one of them had done it. In the morning, and against his host's will as it happened, he had come back. The host had been all sympathy during the night, but as he kept talking about the loss of his family the host's sympathies had faded and Dudley felt pretty sure that the man was partly glad to see him go, no matter what he had said against the move.

As he approached the front of the charred wreck of the main house, he saw Dr. Simmons dusting his trousers with a palm. The doctor had just stepped out of the wreck after a long examination. He looked uncomfortable. His curly mustaches seemed frozen with horror and his sideburns seemed to have wilted in despair.

"I'm sorry about what happened," Simmons began in his usual pompous way. "A very bad business."

"I suppose you've found the bodies," Dudley said, referring to his wife and daughter. Simmons had treated Leola not long ago when she had become ill.

The doctor said grimly, "I could hardly help it. They're almost everywhere along what's left of the place, it would seem."

"Not those. I'm referring to my family."

"Oh." Simmons glanced back of him and made a face. "Could we get a little further away from here, Mr. Stark? The smell of burnt flesh is hard to bear, especially for somebody who's just been poking around in the ruins."

Dudley was too exhausted to care one way or the other, but he followed Dr. Simmons along the scorched ground a little distance to the top of a rise.

"Your wife, I'm sorry to say," Dr. Simmons began, "perished in the fire."

Dudley nodded listlessly. He knew that the pain of it would set in afterwards.

"She died on the instant," Simmons added. "There was no pain."

"Then she hadn't been—hurt."

"Not in any way, no. I'm quite sure of that." Dr. Simmons wouldn't have told Dudley the details of what had been done to Nettie Stark before her death, not if he himself had been tortured.

"You can get those remains separated from the rest, I suppose," Dudley said. "Please do it. We'll talk about burial later on."

"Certainly."

"And the same with my daughter."

"Pardon?" Simmons looked confused. "Miss Leola's body isn't in the house."

"It's on the grounds, then. What difference does it make where the body has been found?"

"No, Mr. Stark, not on the grounds, either. I've been all over Safe Harbor in my wagon and I stopped to look at various points in great detail. I'll take my oath that Miss Leola's body isn't on the premises."

"What? You mean she might be alive?" He remembered Nettie's fears about Leola last night. "Tell me this. Was one of the dead slaves a big powerful man with a skin black as pitch?"

"Most of the skins have been burnt away or charred, but I'd say that the slave you're describing is extraordinary, and no slave who fits that description in height and strength was found on the premises. Slaves don't get fed so well as to become powerful, which always seems to me to be bad business because it takes more men to do as much work as—well, never mind that. It's the wrong time to bring up that point, I'm afraid."

But Stark had hardly been listening. It had to be that Leola had gone off with the slave. It simply had to be!

Galvanized now, and without another word to the astonished Simmons, Dudley ran to his wagon. He started off in the direction of the nearest town, Brayton. It made no sense that the two of them would go there, as Hannibal was wanted for murder in that town. All the same, it might be possible to get some help there, and the two of them may have decided that they could do the same thing.

He wanted to ask the people at the first farmhouse he reached whether or not they had seen Leola and the slave, but decided against it. The place was shuttered and he'd probably have had a hard time getting the people awake.

At the next farmhouse, though, the owner fairly waved Dudley's wagon to a stop. He was a middle-aged man who smoked a pipe with tobacco that smelled almost as bad as the ruins of Safe Harbor.

"Pardon me, Mr. Stark, but I've seen you at town meetings so I know who you are," the man said. "My name is Porter and I want to tell you how sorry I am about what happened to your wife."

"Thank you," Dudley said stiffly. He paused. "I'd like to ask if—"

"It must be some comfort that your daughter is well," Porter said as Dudley became too tongue-tied to go on. "And at least one slave escaped the fire."

Dudley forgot his unwillingness to bring the subject into the open. "Where did you see my daughter?"

"She and the slave were on their way to town, I believe, but she was hungry and they dropped in to ask us for something to eat. My missus and I were only too happy, of course, to oblige her."

"And the slave was a huge black? Yes, I thought so. I suppose you don't have any idea where they were headed for, Mr. Porter? Where in Brayton, I mean."

"Not the slightest, I'm afraid."

"You've been a big help to me, Porter, and I'm obliged to you for it."

Dudley's horse was near exhaustion when he arrived at Brayton, and he left horse and wagon at a blacksmith's. The smith, a huge man with a beard down to his chest, wasn't much of a talker.

Dudley asked, "Which is the best boarding house in town?"

"No idea."

"Who does know?"

"The constable, I guess."

The town constable said that Mrs. Leach's boarding house was the best. And he wanted to offer his condolences to Mr. Stark and his family condolences as well.

Dudley, who hadn't realized that he was expected to receive sympathy whether he wanted it or not, snorted and left. He found Mrs. Leach to be a heavy but friendly woman.

"I'm sorry about your trouble, Mr. Stark," she said as they sat comfortably in her parlor. "I heard about it from —one minute. Was it your daughter who came here yesterday?"

"I believe it was," Dudley nodded. It was good that Leola picked the best place in town. "She was with a black, a slave of ours."

"Yes." Mrs. Leach's voice suddenly grew frosty. "I do believe that what happened to you, the total loss of your property and slaves, was an act of divine retribution against you for owning slaves. God wanted you to see the folly of your ways. I can only hope that never again will you descend to such an abyss of depravity by owning your fellow human beings."

"Madam, let us not discuss the rights and wrongs of the institution," Dudley said, his temper barely controlled. "If God had wanted to strike out at a slave owner, he would have picked one with many more slaves in his pens and who treated his slaves cruelly. If God wanted to strike out at me directly, He would have killed me and not my dear wife. If He killed her in order to make me suffer, then He is a fool."

"God is not mocked," Mrs. Leach said severely.

"He is not respected, either. At least not by me. Not after a senseless tragedy that destroyed a good woman and made her last moments on earth a sheer blazing hell. Now Mrs. Leach, I am not here to discuss the ways of God and man. Would you be kind enough to tell my daughter that I am here?"

"Your daughter isn't staying with me," Mrs. Leach said calmly. "She came here to ask for a room, but I wouldn't let her keep the slave on my grounds. As I say, I am bitterly opposed to slavery and always will be."

"And as a result of your principles, my daughter didn't

209

have any place to sleep last night." Dudley sniffed. "Not to mention the slave whose life you appear to value so highly. All the unhappiness in this world is caused by reformers."

"I sent your daughter off to the Brattle place," Mrs. Leach said. "I felt sure the Brattles wouldn't be so strict."

Dudley left without thanking the woman. He felt sure he would have liked her if she hadn't been such a fool on one subject, and it came to him with a shock that he was already thinking about another wife. Part of him wanted to punish Nettie's memory because Nettie had left him, and part of him felt guilty for having outlived her. He didn't suppose he would ever understand it to his satisfaction.

There was a general store just before he reached the Brattles', and he stopped off. The proprietor was a friendly man who recognized him, and Stark had to endure another round of condolences from strangers.

"What can I do for you, Mr. Stark?" the proprietor said when he had expressed the regrets of himself, his wife, their six children, and by implication the sympathies also of their two dogs and one cat and a parrot and a bowl of goldfish.

"I need some ammunition for this," Dudley said and drew out the pistol.

"Going hunting to forget your troubles?" the proprietor asked affably as he supplied the hardware.

Dudley, who had no intention of leaving the cause of his troubles alive, nodded softly when he thought of a bullet finally piercing Hannibal's huge body.

"I suppose you might say that."

The Brattles, whose boarding house was smaller than that of Mrs. Leach, welcomed him. The wife kept busy working while Brattle invited him into the sun parlor for a little talk. There was another boarder in the sun parlor, but Brattle looked so pained at having his privacy disturbed that the boarder walked off and into another room.

Dudley had to wait till Brattle had expressed regrets and he had thanked him.

"Is my daughter here?" he asked. "She came with a slave."

"Your daughter? Yes, a lovely young lady. Charming, yes, distinctively charming. She should make you a proud grandfather in no time."

He didn't understand why his guest suddenly looked furious.

"Miss Leola Stark, yes," Brattle continued. "She just returned a little while ago from a ride through town, so I know she's upstairs in her room. My dear wife will be only too glad to take you to her."

"Just a moment, please." Dudley hesitated. "Where have you put the slave?"

"Oh, he's in the stable."

"I'll go to him first."

"My dear wife will be glad to show you the way—"

"I can find it." Dudley wouldn't trust himself not to kill the slave as soon as he saw that black devil. "Won't be a minute, Brattle."

"Whatever you like," Brattle said courteously. "I'll tell your daughter that you're here, or rather my dear wife will go upstairs and do that."

"There's no need for that," Dudley said, forcing a smile to his lips. "I'll take care of it all and save your good wife the trouble."

"My wife won't mind at all," Brattle said generously.

"All the same, I'll take care of it myself."

The stable turned out to be a big barn of a place at the back of the house. There were horses and wagons in it, including one freshly lathered animal. There was no sign of Hannibal.

As he left the stable, glancing upstairs at as many of the

211

house windows as he could make out, he was touched by a beefy hand on the shoulder. Dudley whirled around, pistol out, only to see the town constable.

The officer looked at the pistol and said softly, "It occurs to me, Mr. Stark, that the two of us may have come here on the same business."

"I don't know what you're talking about."

"That black nigger bastard was seen driving your daughter through town today," the constable said. "He's wanted for murder, and I plan to get him. It looks as if you've got some plans of your own."

"I came to see my daughter."

"She's not living in the stable," the constable said bluntly.

"What makes you think you can take this tone with me?" Dudley snapped.

"Mr. Stark, we can be honest with each other. You want to get that slave of yours, too. You didn't know he was so valuable till a little while ago and now you need the money so you want to pick up the reward. I don't altogether blame you, Mr. Stark, but I'm a poor man myself. With five hundred dollars, I could make a first payment on a place as big as this one."

As if to prove his point, he gestured toward the house and swept his hand upwards to show its size. He suddenly stopped with the hand in mid-air.

"He's up there. I saw him against the window curtains."

"The nigger?" Dudley put his hand to the pistol. "My daughter is probably giving him instructions about some matter she wants him to attend to. I'm sure she doesn't know what he's done in this town."

"Of course that's it." The constable looked slyly at Dudley Stark, "Are you planning to go upstairs at about this time, Mr. Stark? To straighten your daughter out, I mean."

"I am, yes." Dudley Stark had already begun walking to the back entrance of the house.

"Then I think I'll come with you."

"That won't be necessary." Dudley sighed. "I'll see to it that you get any reward for the nigger. That's a promise. But in return, I want to go up alone. Is that clear?"

"Very well, Mr. Stark, in the circumstances. I'll wait below."

Dudley let himself into the Brattle house, and walked the creaking stairs. There was a window that let him see a view of the restless constable as he walked. Dudley could hear the Brattles in the kitchen, talking, not knowing about the violence that was soon going to be visited on their house.

His heart was hammering against his chest, and a fine coating of sweat lined his face and hands. He gripped the pistol as he walked from one door to the next, listening for his daughter and the nigger. He hoped it was possible that he'd hear something besides the creak of a mattress or the scream of his child as she was attacked by the black man.

He was faced by two rows of five black doors with white paint in a frame on each. With an ear against one door from which he had detected sounds, he heard a man and woman in a bitter argument. At another door he heard a man singing *Rock of Ages* in a high clear voice. He stepped in front of a third door just as that boarder stepped out of it and gave Dudley a suspicious look. Dudley had to make believe he was a new boarder looking for his own door and who had mistaken another one for it. The boarder glared at him as he passed.

In front of one door he heard a voice that sounded as though it belonged to a Negro, but he had to walk ahead. The old boarder finally went down the stairs, and Dudley returned swiftly and silently to the door from which he had heard the Negro man's voice.

213

It wasn't Hannibal, but an older Negro who was apparently talking to his wife. They were free, it seemed. Dudley sighed and passed on.

He heard a mattress creaking at the next door and knew it was the right one. He didn't have any real reason to know, but he felt certain. He never had any idea how he controlled himself and kept from beating the door down. Maybe it was the one-in-a-million chance that he might be mistaken which restrained him or the recollection of recent embarrassment.

He expected to hear his daughter moan in agony and shame and humiliation; at the first sound of her pain-filled voice he would shoot the lock off the door.

Instead he listened as his daughter said invitingly:

"Just one time can't hurt either of us, darling."

Dismayed and stunned, Dudley hoped against hope that she was there with, at the very least, a white man.

But it was Hannibal, the slave named Hannibal, who said, "Haven't I done enough for you already?"

Dudley gripped his pistol, prepared to shoot off the lock and to destroy Hannibal as soon as he was inside. He kept from doing it when he heard his daughter say: "I know you saved my life in the troubles at Safe Harbor and I know you saved me from being humiliated by some of those vile blacks up there. I realize that if not for you, Hannibal, I wouldn't be alive today."

Confusion and deep anger kept Dudley where he was. For a moment he hoped he wasn't breathing so heavily that they would hear him. Only for a moment, till he got his strength back. He could smell the sharp disinfectant on the floor and the dust spots that danced and whirled around him.

Leola was saying, "I know I owe you everything, and I can't really pay you back, but I hoped you might want to—well, you know."

He must have known. And Dudley knew, too.

"No, I—I have to go now." The slave sounded hurried. "They promised to take me out of here soon as possible, and I want to get up North. I want to get away from Alabama and everything it means."

"I can understand that, of course," Leola said sadly. "But you didn't mind at all when I practically forced you to give me some part of you that first time back at Safe Harbor."

Dudley was immobile now, forcing himself to stay where he was and not move.

"And you felt the same when I practically made you do it to me the second time. All I'm asking you to do now is to take fifteen or twenty minutes to love me. We'll spend the rest of our lives apart and never see each other again."

"No, Miss, I can't do that."

Dudley Stark never knew why he did what he did in the next few minutes. He would go to his grave in the year 1860 without the slightest idea what made him behave as he did at that particular moment or why. He would reach a point in life, seeing his daughter unhappily married to the rich drunkard who had given him a loan to build up Safe Harbor once again, when he denied to himself that he had ever gone against the training of a lifetime. He couldn't possibly have done something that contradicted everything he stood for.

"Did I do that?" Dudley Stark would ask himself when old age had crept up over him and he would wake up in the middle of the night and see his second wife fast asleep. "Could I really have done all that?"

For Dudley Stark began by raising his pistol and shooting the lock off the door. Ignoring the noise and stench of cordite, he knocked the door off its hinges.

Only out of the corner of an eye did he see his own daughter suddenly cover herself in the bed and see the slave, fully clothed and with jaw dropping, stare at him.

Knowing that the town constable waited outside and

215

near the barn, Dudley fired his second shot through the window, smashing glass. Then, skirting the slave gingerly, Dudley ran to the other end of the room and turned. The slave, jaw still fallen, looked in frantic hope to the door. The damn fool couldn't bring himself to move, though, and Dudley wouldn't say a direct word or make a motion to show what he wanted Hannibal to do. He considered that much as a point of honor.

"I've got you now," Dudley shouted triumphantly so that the constable would hear. "My gun is pointed straight at your nigger heart."

But his gun was pointed down at the floor.

"You can't run out the front way now, boy, no matter how quiet you try to be," Dudley kept on shouting. "I'm gonna hang you, boy. Understand that? I'm going to take you right outside to the barn where the town constable is waiting, and me and him are going to hang you by your black dirty damn neck."

The boy was nobody's fool, Dudley was glad to see. Silently he ran to the door, then turned back as if he could hardly believe he hadn't been shot. For the first time and the last, the two men looked directly at each other. No word or gesture passed between them. At no time did Hannibal show by look or deed that the white man who had hunted him all the time had actually saved his life. At no time did Dudley Stark look for gratitude from the black man, nor would he have accepted it with anything but a snarl.

And then the moment was over. Hannibal was running silently along the hall and down the stairs—running to a freedom which would bring him pain and disappointments, but not regret.

Dudley took it for granted that nobody in the house had been willing to venture so close to the sound of gunfire. He felt drained and terribly tired.

He didn't look at his daughter, but said to her, "I'll wait for you downstairs."

He walked down quietly and stiffly, not able to keep from believing what he had heard or accept what he had done. The constable came rushing into the hall from the back entrance.

"What happened? I saw you walking down by yourself after all that shouting. Where's the nigger?"

"Gone."

"Was he that streak I saw flashing past the window? Musta been, I guess." His face became purple. "But the reward money—what about that?"

Dudley looked tired. "I'll make it up to you as soon as Safe Harbor is on its feet again. That's a promise."

He felt terribly tired, and as if he wanted to spend his life righting wrongs and easing pain. For if he had been so mistaken about Hannibal, didn't it seem reasonable that he was mistaken about other black men and women, too? At least about some others.

He wandered into the parlor, where Mr. Brattle sat rigid. At Dudley's first question, he announced that his wife had gone next door to look for help. Dudley offered to pay the money that Leola owed. Brattle took it absently and stowed it into a small pocket. Dudley doubted whether Mrs. Brattle would ever see a penny of it.

"Brattle," Dudley asked absently, "did you ever feel that your whole life had been a mistake? That the things you'd always believed might all along have been wrong?"

Brattle found his voice with difficulty. "Yes, sir, I've often felt that way."

"And what did you do about it?"

"Why, sir," Brattle said slowly, "I would go to the saloon and have myself another drink."

Dudley did not smile. He left the Brattle place with his daughter. In the wagon, he told her what had happened at Safe Harbor, but didn't use one word of endearment or sympathy.

A crew of white workmen rebuilt the main house, and Dudley made a point of furnishing it as before. He hired a new overseer and gave instructions about being fair and decent and gentle with the slaves he had bought at New Orleans. They were to be well-fed, well-housed and well-treated. The whipping post had been torn down during the riot, and Dudley wouldn't hear of putting up a new one.

But his overseer quit the job in three months, saying that it was impossible to work well under the restrictions that Dudley had set.

"The cotton isn't being planted quick enough," the overseer said as he resigned. "The slaves won't work and as there's no discipline there isn't any way to make 'em work. Furthermore, we've had runaways by the dozens."

"Thank you, Page," Dudley said rigidly. "Stay for two weeks, and that'll give me time enough to hire a new man."

He repeated his instructions to the new overseer, who looked the place over and suggested a whipping post be put up.

"Very well," Dudley gave in. "But it's not to be used. I don't want to hear that it's been used."

"You won't hear, Mister Stark," the overseer promised.

In six months, though, that overseer was running Safe Harbor as swiftly and efficiently as Joe Everdine had done, and Dudley Stark concerned himself no further in the day-to-day treatment of slaves.

CHAPTER 23

Hannibal settled in Boston and wrote to Cindy at the address she had given him. That is, he paid somebody to write the letter. Cindy joined him in a month. They stayed together for a year, and then decided to get married. For a while, Cindy worked as a maid. Hannibal had got a job as a hod carrier and he made a good living at it. He worked hard, and after a day on the job he could do what he wanted. He wasn't living with his wife in any slave pens, either.

Cindy stopped working when she gave birth to their first child. Hannibal had said that if it was a boy he would want it named Dudley after the white man who had owned him and given him freedom.

"You want to name a son of ours after a white man?" Cindy demanded incredulously. "And a slave owner to boot?"

"Without him, I wouldn't be free."

"Not after a white man," Cindy said firmly, shaking her head.

Their first child was a daughter, as was their second. The third was a son, however, which started the argument all over again. Cindy got the name "Harold" onto the baby's birth certificate, but Hannibal kept calling him "Dudley," and she finally gave in. The certificate was changed.

Young Dudley enlisted in the Army during the Civil War, as soon as the Army had started to accept Negroes.

Hannibal and Cindy saw the lad off to war and so did his girl friend, Dorothea. Cindy, who had never been a religious woman, took to praying for the lad.

Hannibal's son had the great good fortune to come back alive and whole, which many of the soldiers in his regiment didn't do. At a family party to which Dorothea and her folks had been invited, the boy talked about his experiences. He had seen slave pens and had talked to many former slaves. He couldn't stop talking about the way they had lived and how bone-ignorant they were and how much he hated them for having let themselves be destroyed by the whites. Hannibal glowered at the boy until he finally said that his dad, at least, had run off.

"Were you in Alabama?" he asked the boy.

"Sure was. There was one place we saw called Bon Repos and a white man named Colin Ramsey, who had lost both legs and tried to fire on us. Somebody shot and killed him."

"What about Safe Harbor? That's where I—I had to work."

"I remember you telling me about it," young Dudley said. "When our troops reached it there was nobody in charge. I told 'em that it was where my father'd had to be a slave and I wanted to get even for you. So we all burned the place to the ground. We didn't leave none of it to stand up."

Hannibal felt stunned. Was Safe Harbor going to be destroyed and built up again every few years?

"The South is in ruins," young Dudley said with the assurance of youth. "We smashed it, destroyed it, tore it to pieces and stamped on the pieces. It'll never be the same again. It'll never rise. Every white man and woman in the South has got just what you and the other slaves must have always wished on them."

It was true, of course, and the sort of news Hannibal had always told himself he wanted to hear: the white

220

man humbled, the cotton crop worthless, the white man ruined and in rags, starving, living in the slave pens because only the slave pens had been left standing.

But Hannibal looked at his eager and pleased young son and wondered why the news didn't make him happy.